BLOOD CROSSED

NETHERWORLD PARANORMAL POLICE DEPARTMENT: BOOK ONE

JOHN P. LOGSDON

CHRISTOPHER P. YOUNG

D1522366

CRIMSON MYTH
PRESS

Published by: Crimson Myth Press (www.CrimsonMyth.com)

Cover art: Audrey Logsdon (www.AudreyLogsdon.com)

Thanks to TEAM ASS!
Advanced Story Squad

This is the first line of readers of the series. Their job is to help me keep things in check and also to make sure I'm not doing anything way off base in the various story locations!

(listed in alphabetical order by first name)

Adam Saunders-Pederick
Bennah Phelps
Debbie Tily
Hal Bass
Helen Suanders-Pederick
John Debnam
Larry Diaz Tushman
Marie McCraney
Mike Helas
Natalie Fallon
Noah Sturdevant
Paulette Kilgore
Penny Campbell-Myhill
Scott Reid

Thanks to Team DAMN
Demented And Magnificently Naughty

This crew is the second line of readers who get the final draft of the story, report any issues they find, and do their best to inflate my fragile ego.

(listed in alphabetical order by first name)

Adam Goldstein, Allen Stark, Amanda Holden, Amy Robertson, Andrew Greeson, Bennah Phelps, Beth Adams, Bonnie Dale Keck, Brandy Dalton, Carolyn Fielding, Carolyn Jean Evans, Charlotte Webby, Christopher Ridgway, Dan Sippel, David Botell, Denise King, Heather Holden, Helen Day, Ian Nick Tarry, Jacky Oxley, Jamie Gray, Jan Gray, Jim Stoltz, Jodie Stackowiak, Kathleen Portig, Kathryne Nield, Kevin Frost, Laura Stoddart, Lucas Warwick, Mark Junk, Mary Letton, MaryAnn Sims, Megan McBrien, Megan Thigpen, Michelle Reopel, Myles Mary Cohen, Pete Sandry, Ruth Nield, Sandee Lloyd, Sara Pateman, Sharon Robb, Steve Woofie Widner, Tehrene Hart.

I'd faced down vampires and werewolves and everything else over my time as a Retriever in the Netherworld PPD, but this was the first time I'd been saddled with a rookie.

His name was Reaper Payne and he was tall, lanky, had glowing eyes, and a perpetual five-o-clock shadow. He also wore a long black coat and a leather cowboy hat. He looked a bit out of place, truth be told.

Unfortunately, that was all the information I had on him because Chief Carter pushed the guy off on me seconds before a Retriever call came in.

"He's inside," I said, pointing at the Apollo Marine Specialties building on Lesseps Street in New Orleans, Louisiana. We were standing across the road, hidden in the shadows. "Get your gun ready."

"I don't have a gun," he replied, glancing over at me.

I looked at him in disbelief.

"So you're a cop with no gun?" I shook my head, thinking about how the chief and I were going to have to have a talk about things. "Okay, rookie, first rule of law enforcement is that when you're chasing the bad guys, you bring a gun."

"I use magic," he deadpanned.

"You're a mage?"

"No, I'm a reaper."

I squinted with one eye while raising my opposite eyebrow.

"You mean one of the guys who brings the dead to the…whatever you call it?"

"Yes."

A sound came from inside the building. Something had fallen. It was obvious that our rogue vampire was fishing around in there. We hadn't tipped our hand with him yet, so he couldn't have known we were after him.

"Did you get laid off or something?" I asked as I pulled out my spare gun and went to hand it to him.

"Again, Ms. Shaw, I don't use guns," he said, looking down at it. "They're an abomination."

"So is being shredded by a vampire," I replied. Then I grimaced at the "Ms. Shaw" reference. "And don't call me that. It makes me feel like I'm an old maid."

"Officer Shaw, then," he started again, "I do not use guns because—"

"Just call me Piper," I interrupted. "I'll call you Reap."

"I would prefer 'Officer Payne.'"

I laughed. "Yeah, like I'm going to run around calling you Officer Payne."

The image of me arresting some poor old wizard who had accidentally missed his return trip to the Netherworld came to mind. *'Sorry, sir, but you'll have to come with us, and don't make things difficult or I'll send Officer Payne to teach you a lesson!'*

"I'm going to stick with Reap or Payne or whatever else strikes my mood." That's when a thought hit me. "Wait a second," I said as I stuck the spare gun back in its holster, "are you telling me that you're a reaper whose name is Reaper?"

"That's correct."

"Are all reapers named Reaper or are you just the least creative of the bunch?"

His eyes glowed a little brighter.

"We don't have names in the same fashion as you do, Offic...Piper," he replied evenly. "We merely sense each other as unique."

"Sounds lovely," I replied. "Of course there is the matter of your last name."

"Yes, I have been in the Netherworld for quite some time. One has to acclimate, so I adopted a last name."

"And you chose 'Payne?'" There was no response to that. "Anyway, how about turning down your headlights there a bit so our fun-loving vampire doesn't spot us?"

His eyes dimmed. "Nobody has ever mentioned the brightness of my eyes being a problem."

"That's because everyone is too worried about being politically correct," I scoffed. "You'll soon find out that I'm not one who buys into that crap. If you're doing something stupid that might get us in trouble, I'll tell you."

"And my eyes are stupid?"

"When they're glowing like the sun while we're sneaking around, yeah."

There was one more thing bugging me about him.

Shouldn't a reaper have some type of archaic speech patterns? My assumption was that he'd also gotten up to speed with that over his years living here.

There was a crack from inside the building.

It was time to move.

"All right," I said in a commanding voice, "here's how it's going to work. You're going to go that way,"—I pointed—"and I'm going to cut straight across. You're acting as backup, got it?"

"Yes."

"If there's any trouble, just cast a lightning bolt or something at the guy..." I stopped. "Assuming I haven't already shot him, I mean."

"I don't cast lightning bolts."

"An ice barrage, then," I said, not really caring.

"Can't do that either," he replied while looking at his feet.

I took a step toward the building but paused and looked back.

"Fireball?"

He nodded. "That, I can do."

"Swell."

I hid the gun behind my back and casually crossed the street, just a little to the left of the entryway. I also made it look like I was planning to walk down and away from the building.

As soon as I got to the other side, though, I pinned my back to the wall beside the door and got ready for a fight.

Reaper was heading toward me, his eyes glowing like a couple of car lights. If the chief stuck him with me for the long haul—something I planned to argue against—I was going to have to get him some shades.

Sinking down, I peered through the open door and spotted a body. She was lying only a few feet inside.

Our vampire was feeding.

Well, that was fun. It meant he had additional strength and agility. I looked at my gun, thinking it was nothing a Death Nail couldn't stop, but seeing that Reaper was against the use of guns, I'd have to make sure the vampire didn't get hold of him.

"Eyes," I hissed as Reaper got to the other side of the door.

They dimmed.

And here came the part of the job that I felt was incredibly stupid. Unfortunately, it was a highly recommended practice for each Retriever. It was supposed to protect us from a countersuit in the event the perp we were arresting got injured while apprehending. I didn't do it all the time, but seeing that Reaper was new, I thought it a smart move.

I sighed and then called out, "Gallien Cross, by order of the Netherworld Retrievers, I, Piper Shaw, and my partner, Reaper Payne, hereby place you under arrest, and we shall transport you back to the Netherworld and present you before the Tribunal for sentencing."

Usually the response to this was one of three things. The most common was the runner yelling "Fuck you!" before attacking me. The second was a sobbing sound followed by a long diatribe explaining why they had run in the first place. And the last was resignation to the fact that they weren't getting out of this, meaning that they'd just walk out with their hands up.

Gallien's response was new, though.

An Empiric came flying out the door, landing directly between me and Reaper.

"Oh, shit," I said as I dived as far away as possible.

CHAPTER 2

*T*he explosion was deadened pretty heavily, which was odd.

An Empiric was essentially a magical grenade. It was shaped like a disc that was about an inch high with a two-inch circumference. They were made of a black alloy that popped open when activated, revealing a blue light that spun in on itself until throwing out a massive magical shockwave, killing pretty much anything in its path.

Anything not immortal anyway. Fortunately—or maybe not, depending on the day, I *was* immortal. So getting hit by an Empiric wouldn't kill me, but it'd still hurt like hell, hence why I dived away.

But not feeling *anything* from one was odd. There should have at least been a concussive "boom."

"Ouch," I heard Reaper say, and I pushed myself up and turned around.

He was lying on top of the Empiric and his long coat did not look happy about it.

"What the fuck?" I breathed as I darted over and

pushed him onto his back. "Are you okay?"

"That hurt a fair bit," he replied, swallowing, "but I'll be okay. Just need a minute to heal."

I didn't see any holes in his chest, but his shirt was completely destroyed. There were some burn marks, too, but they seemed to be healing already. That just meant he still had his reaper immortality, regardless of his new position in the Netherworld.

"Why would you throw yourself on an Empiric, Reap?" I asked. "That's just insane."

"I was trying to protect you and the people in the area," he answered.

That made my eye twitch. Was he thinking of me as some kind of damsel in distress? If so, I'd have to kick him in the nuts a few times to demonstrate that I was more than capable of taking care of myself.

I cracked my neck from side to side.

"So the big man has to protect the little woman? Is that what you're telling me?"

My foot was ready to swing.

"Not at all," he replied, his glowing eyes meeting my non-glowing ones. "I was assigned as your partner. If you were a man, I would have done the same thing."

I held my foot back.

"Okay, then." My angst lowered. "Well, thanks, but that was stupid."

"You're welcome." He pushed himself up with some effort.

"And that brings us to rule number two of retrieving runners," I said as I glanced into the building. "Do you remember rule number one?"

"Bring a gun," he replied with a sigh.

I tilted my head at him. "Good. Rule number two is that you don't throw yourself on a fucking Empiric." I grew pedantic. "Now, I know they don't point these things out in cop-school, so learn from my experience."

"What happens if we let an Empiric explode unabated, Piper?" he asked as he rubbed his chest.

"It makes a big boom and kills a bunch..." I looked around and noticed there were a few normals milling about on the streets. "Okay, I see your point, but there are better ways to destroy an Empiric."

"In less than three seconds?"

He had me there. "Well, no, but that's not the point."

"What *is* the point, then?"

"Just that you shouldn't throw yourself on an Empiric," I replied, and then I stepped inside the building while keeping my gun up. "It's moronic."

The room was clear, except for the woman's body I'd seen before Gallien's attack.

"By the way," I said as Reaper knelt beside the woman, "that's rule number three: Don't be a moron."

He rolled his eyes at me, which was only obvious because his pupils were slightly brighter than the rest of his eyes.

"Just so you're aware," he said, "I have seen more death in one day than you'll see in a lifetime."

"Well, I'm an immortal, so don't get too high on yourself."

"And how long have you been alive, exactly?"

"Twenty-seven years, but—"

"Right, so you're still very young. I've been a reaper for

millennia and seeing death is nonstop. It kind of goes with the job."

He focused his attention back on the body on the floor.

I stuck my tongue out at him and then flipped over my left arm and tapped the tattoo on my wrist. It was shaped like two sets of horns that were connected at the base in the middle, slanting slightly away from each other. There were lines from the outer horns that angled into the centers of the inner horns as well. By placing the fingers of my right hand in various locations, and using specific sequences, I could trigger a ton of functions that would appear in my field of vision. I could also control the tattoo with my mind if I had to, but it wasn't easy and it required going into a light trance.

The tracking system showed that Gallien had crossed the train tracks and was heading into a building by the Mississippi.

I sighed.

On the one hand, it wasn't like he'd get out of our sight anytime soon because we could track him; on the other hand, he'd clearly killed one normal already, so we needed to stop him before he did it again.

"Dead?" I asked as I came back to Reaper and the body.

"Technically, I'm neither dead nor alive," Reaper replied.

"Not you, bozo," I said, frowning. "I'm talking about her."

"Oh, right. Not yet." He had his left hand on her forehead while making various gestures with his right. "I'm putting her in stasis and will send her to Dr. Hale's office for healing." He looked up. "Assuming it's not too late."

I nodded. If anyone could revive the woman, it'd be the good doctor in the Netherworld PPD.

The interesting bit, though, was that Reaper was putting the lady in stasis. That could be pretty useful. There were countless times I could recall when a normal had been down and out due to a werewolf bite or a mage firing an energy bolt through them. They usually lasted a few minutes before giving up the ghost. Reaper's little trick could extend that quite a bit.

That made me look at Reaper again. If anyone knew about giving up the ghost, I guessed it'd be him.

"How long is it going to take?" I asked. "I'm tracking Gallien, but it'd be better if he didn't strike again."

"Nearly done."

"Good."

I pulled out the Death Nail I had sticking in the lining of my belt and looked it over. I always kept one hidden there in case I ever got captured and had my gun stripped away. Death Nails were interesting bullets that were developed specifically for killing supernaturals. They were nasty. When one struck a supernatural, it divided itself over and over, sending various metals and earthen elements through the target. Like tiny explosions within explosions. Within seconds, the creature was decimated. If it hit a normal, it was like getting shot by a one-inch nail, meaning that it would still hurt like hell and *could* kill if it hit the wrong spot, but it wouldn't divide and spread elements throughout the body.

"Sending her through now," Reaper announced as he ran his fingers over his tattoo.

The body faded from view and he stood up somewhat wobbly.

"You okay?" I asked, reaching over to steady him.

"Yes. I just get a little dizzy when I use my powers."

"Do all reapers have this stasis power and such?" I asked as we stepped outside and started heading down to the docks.

All PPD officers could send people to the Netherworld in emergency, or if they were delivering bad people to jail, but stasis was not something I'd seen before.

"No," he answered while flipping his arm over to reveal that his tattoo ran farther up than mine, "those powers come from my Pecker-issued artwork."

He was referring to our technician, Rube Pecker. The guy was a whiz at technology. He was also one of the few goblins working in the precinct. I enjoyed his accent, which reminded me of the people in New York.

I studied Reaper's ink. It was identical to mine at the top, but there were several tendrils that rolled down his arm toward his bicep. Each appendage split into different directions, with some of them connecting farther down.

"I didn't know Pecker could do that," I said.

"Technically, he could only do that with me," he replied. "I have a unique energy signature that allows for it."

"Well, aren't you special?"

"Lucky, I guess."

I pointed at his other arm. "What's with the Mala bracelet?"

"Also due to my particular energy signature. If I try to go through the portal system without that, I can become quite damaged."

"Why?"

"I don't know, but I learned about it the hard way. It was not a fun couple of weeks, I assure you." He played with the strings on the bracelet. "Dr. Hale thought I was going to actually die, though I assured her that was unlikely."

"Well, it looks rather manly." I coughed.

"What's wrong with it?" he said, looking down at the bracelet with concern. "It's got black beads and there's skulls on it and everything."

"Oh, well, there you go then."

I ran another check on the position of Gallien and found that he was in the first building. He wasn't moving around very much, so he was either waiting for us or he had lopped his arm off so we couldn't track him.

Every supernatural was marked in order to be trackable. We knew where everyone was at all times. It was part of the deal when moving around in the Overworld. So wherever Gallien's wrist went, we'd know. Even more important was the fact that he was an escaped prisoner, and inmates had enhancers set on their transmitters in case they got away.

We crossed the tracks, got to the building, and began scooting along the outer walls toward the river side, taking it slow in case Gallien had any nefarious traps planned.

It was go time.

CHAPTER 3

*T*he place was dark as I peered around, not wanting to fully commit to entering just yet.

I glanced back and noted that Reaper had his eyebeams set to low.

"Can't you shut your eyes off completely?"

"No."

I sniffed and then got to work.

"Come on out, Gallien," I called as we stood on either side of the entrance. "There's no other exit, and if you throw another fucking grenade at me I'll cut your balls open and soak them in pickle juice."

Reaper whispered in an admonishing way, "Really?"

"What?" I said over my shoulder. "I'd do it."

"I've no doubt of that, but is it really necessary to speak in such a fashion?"

Who was he to judge my methods?

"Fuck you," I said seriously.

"I'll take that as a yes."

Gallien hadn't replied to my request, which meant we had to enter the building.

We slowly made our way just inside the door, where we found Gallien waiting for us. He was standing about halfway to the back of the open space, his arms crossed. He was also wearing that same grin he'd held before.

"Where did you get an Empiric?" I questioned, my gun pointed at his head.

"I found it lying in the grass," Gallien replied with a sneer. "Seems lucky since I needed to defend myself against you two clowns." He looked over at Reaper. "Nice glowing eyes, by the way. If you're going to do this line of work, you should probably invest in some shades."

"See?" I said, glancing over at my new partner. "Now, Gallien, we never took a single shot at you. Besides, using that type of firepower up here is going to land you in jail for a solid twenty years, which will be tacked on to the ten you're already looking at for escaping." I scanned the area, but couldn't see past him. The windows near the back of the tall ceiling were streaming in a nice dose of moonlight, but everything under about ten feet was pitch black. It wasn't so much an absence of light, but more like the light was being consumed. "Now, if you come along nicely, I may convince myself that the Empiric was just an unfortunate mistake on your part," I said as the hairs on the back of my neck stood on end. "If you don't, then you'll get the full rap at your trial."

"Let's not forget the young lady he bit," Reaper noted.

"Valid point," I said with a nod and then turned back to Gallien and shrugged. "I kind of have to bring that up, I'm afraid."

"It's a shame that the Empiric didn't destroy you two idiots." He was too damn calm. It put me on edge, and I was already on edge, so now I was on the edge of being on the edge. "As for the girl, I was hungry."

Reaper and I took another couple of steps closer. I was keeping my gun trained on Gallien.

"Come on," I said, motioning for him to break out of the shadows. "I'd hate to have to drop a Death Nail in you."

That wasn't true at all. I was rather hoping he'd go to pull a weapon. He was the kind who didn't give two shits about anything or anyone. The world was his to manipulate and punish. In a nutshell, he was a downright douche-canoe.

But my rent was due and I needed a full commission. A dead perp only got me twenty-five percent. I wanted the full bounty.

He glanced down at my gun and looked back at me. Then, he smiled and took a step deeper into the shadows.

He disappeared.

Just as I was about to fire the weapon at the location where he'd been standing, three goons stepped out from different areas of the shadowed wall.

"These are some friends of mine," Gallien called out from a location that was clearly nowhere near where he'd just been. I tried to place it, but the reverb in the room was making it impossible. "They're part of my old gang, and their job is to tie up any inconveniences for me."

The three vampires all held guns of their own.

I was fast, but not that fast.

"Have fun," Gallien said from the shadows.

"I don't see how that's possible," I called back.

Gallien chuckled. "I was talking to my friends."

"Oh, right."

CHAPTER 4

*M*y initial reaction was to dive off to my left and start firing, but I had a feeling Reaper wasn't quite as adept as I was with this sort of thing.

I didn't want to tap around on my wrist in front of these guys so I slowed my mind as I worked to connect with my tattoo. It wasn't as easy for me as it was for others. This was entirely my fault since I hate sitting around learning shit, but it was at times like these when I wished I'd had more patience.

I already knew they were vampires since I had the ability to see supernaturals for what they were. That little skill was how I ended up in this job in the first place, and it was also the reason my parents were killed when I was five. Let's just say that being a normal and having the unique ability to spot supernaturals could put you on the hit list of any super who was up to no good.

Fortunately, I only needed a quick read on their names and records. I looked at each of their faces carefully so that the system could use their visual for a search.

Gunter Stills had gone missing many years ago and was presumed dead because his mark had stopped functioning. Phillip Jameson and Haley Rivers were the same.

Interesting.

"*Reap,*" I said through the connector, which was the device implanted in the brain of every PPD officer so that we could communicate without the need for words and without having to carry around a cell phone, "*ever been in a firefight before?*"

"No," he answered aloud.

Everyone looked at him.

"*Sorry,*" he said, this time through the connector. "*I'm still not used to this thing. Pecker has only recently been able to update my tattoo to use a version of the connector that works for me.*"

"It's not in your head?"

"No." Again, it was said out loud. "*Sorry, no.*"

"Why do you keep saying, 'No?'" asked Haley.

"He does that when he starts getting angry," I said quickly. Then I connected to him again and said, "*Turn up your eyebeams.*"

Fortunately, he didn't question me this time. He just did it.

The three vampires backed away slightly, but I sensed their trigger fingers were even itchier than they'd been before.

"*I'm going to count to three,*" I said, "*when I hit three, you hit the ground, understand?*"

I saw his mouth move, but he then replied affirmatively through the connector.

Progress.

"*One...two...three!*"

I fired off a round as Reaper hit the ground.

It was a perfectly aimed Death Nail that should have hit Phillip in the chest, broken into a flurry of pieces and rattled his insides with mayhem until he died.

Unfortunately, the Nail stopped in mid-air and fell to the ground with a *cling-clang*.

Gunter was grinning from ear to ear as I frowned at the three vampires.

"You must think us stupid, Officer Shaw," he stated.

"Well, yeah," I agreed, "but I don't see what that has to do with anything."

His grin faded.

"Kill her," said Gunter.

I dived toward a box that was off to my left as the bullets began to fly.

There was no chance for me to worry about Reaper at the moment. He was on his own. It wasn't a biggie, though. He'd been able to withstand the power of an Empiric while lying on the damn thing. I doubted standard bullets would do much more than sting a little. Now, if they were using breaker bullets or Death Nails, that'd be diff—

A thud sounded and I looked up to see a Death Nail sticking out of the side of the box.

"*Son of a bitch,*" I said through the connector. "*These bastards have Nails. You might want to get the hell out of here, Reaper.*"

"*I'm safely shielded,*" he replied in a calm voice.

"Oh, well, thanks for thinking about protecting your partner. Truly appreciate the sentiment."

"You dived away before I had the opportunity, I'm afraid." I glanced in his direction as he casually walked toward me. *"There. You're safe now."*

I peeked around the box and saw Death Nails bouncing off the shield and littering the floor.

I stood up, feeling rather pompous indeed. While I hated to admit it, it was nice to have a partner who could put up a shield. That was a luxury I'd never had before.

"Well, Gunter, Phillip, and Haley," I said, holstering my gun, "it seems that we are at a stalemate."

"How do you know our names?" asked Phillip.

"Don't be a fool," Haley spat while giving Phillip a glare. "They're Retrievers."

"I know that, Haley, but we're supposed to be untrackable."

"And you are," I said before Haley could reply, "but you should have changed your appearances, too, or at least have worn masks."

"Damn it," said Phillip.

Gunter was the only one who appeared nonplussed at the fact that I knew who they were. He merely kept his cold stare connected to my eyes as he casually snapped his fingers.

That liquid darkness faded away, revealing a metallic cylinder that I'd seen once before.

It was a Shredder, also known as a Mama Empiric. Basically, you take a bunch of Empirics and put them in one big-ass silver casing.

They go boom.

Big *boom*.

"Is that what I think it is?" asked Reaper, using his outside voice.

"Yep," I said, "and I don't think your shield is going to protect us against that."

"Agreed."

Gunter, Haley, and Phillip backed away toward a door that sat behind the Shredder.

"Goodbye, Officer Shaw," said Gunter coldly. "I do hope you end up in Hell."

"Actually…" Reaper began, but I grabbed him by the arm and started running toward the water.

We jumped in a split-second before the world erupted in flames.

CHAPTER 5

*W*e were soaked and I was annoyed. I hated getting bested, and tonight it'd happened to me twice.

The building was still burning as we climbed out of the water. I stood and stared at the place. This entire thing felt like a setup. But why?

"Is it just me," mused Reaper as he emptied the water from his hat, "or did this feel like they were planning to destroy us?"

"I was just thinking the same thing," I answered, surprised that we were on the same wavelength, especially with him being new to the beat. "I doubt it had anything to do with you, though."

"Why would you think that?"

"Because you don't know any of these guys."

"You do?"

"Not directly, but I've been a Retriever for quite some time. When you throw enough perps in jail, your name gets around."

"I suppose that makes sense."

What I was trying to figure out was why they'd go out of their way to kill me. That made no sense seeing that all it would accomplish was to bring a magnifying glass on them.

Maybe that's precisely what they wanted?

"By the way," I said, unable to keep my trap shut, "would it have killed you to launch a fireball or two at them during the fight?"

"I can't cast one while holding up a shield," he answered.

I wanted to gripe about that, but there wasn't much I could say. Even mages had this issue and they were meant to do magic. Reaper was just a reaper with special tech.

"We need to go back in there," I said, walking toward the burning building.

"Why?"

"Because they're planning something big, that's why. Put up your shield thing so we don't burn."

He did so as the sound of sirens filled the air. Firetrucks were on the way, meaning we only had a couple of minutes before we had to be gone.

I scanned the debris, looking for anything that might clue us in on what Gallien Cross had in mind. The only thing I noticed were the charred remains of a few bodies.

They were normals.

"Four vampires, four bodies," I stated. "That means they're building up strength."

"I only see three bodies," Reaper said while looking around.

"I'm including the one you put in stasis, Reap."

"Ah, right."

The flashing of red and white lights filled the scene as the rumble of big engines and the sound of sirens bounced off the walls.

It was time to go.

"We have to…" I stopped as I spotted something in the corner.

Two runes sat side by side. I could read most runes, but there were some that got a little too complex for me. I couldn't create runes. Well, I suppose I could draw something up, but without the magic in my veins it wouldn't be anything more than a fancy design coming from my fingers.

I pushed the debris out of the way and saw them in their entirety.

"What is it?"

"Veiling rune," I said, pointing at the first one, which explained the absence of light when we'd walked into the place earlier. "That's how they were hiding everything." Then I pointed at the second one, even though Reaper was likely just seeing a blank space on the wall. "And that's a shield."

"Interesting."

"More than you know." I sighed. "It means they have a wizard or a mage on their side."

It was more likely a wizard since mages tended not to dabble in runes that much, but there was one way to find out. Runes were unique, having their own fingerprint, as it were. If I could get a visual of the thing, I could have Pecker run a trace on it. While my eyes worked fine at identifying faces along with my tattoo, it didn't work that way with runes, and I couldn't exactly take a snapshot of the thing because film wouldn't pick it up.

"I don't suppose you have any ideas on how to grab a picture of this?" I said as the sound of voices and pounding feet got closer.

Reaper shook his head. "I can't even see them."

"Damn."

There was nothing around I could use to draw him a sketch. Not that there was time. We had to get out of here before any of the firefighters saw us.

With a groan, I took one last look at the runes and then signaled Reaper that it was time to go.

We both activated our tattoos and transported back into the Netherworld.

CHAPTER 6

"Where's Gallien?" Chief Carter urged, staring us down as we stepped off the transport platform.

Carter was your average, run-of-the-mill cop. He was a mage who was quite old, having gray hair with a matching mustache and beard. He stood around five foot eight and was a bit saggy in the middle. Imagine a short Gandalf, or maybe Santa Claus, and you'll get the idea of it. Nice-enough guy, but he had a tendency of getting edgy when things weren't going his way.

"He skipped out on us," I answered, "after first trying to blow us up with an Empiric, rip us apart with Death Nails, and then shred us with...well, a Shredder."

Carter's eyes went wide at my words.

"That's exactly how I felt, Chief," I said with an empathetic nod. "Also, they had a couple of runes in the warehouse. One was a veiling rune and the other was a shield."

"So they have a wizard helping them," he uttered.

"Or a mage," I pointed out, though I knew he'd already thought of that possibility.

We stepped aside as a couple of cops escorted a partially morphed werewolf past us.

The Netherworld PPD was built like any police station you might find in the Overworld. There were desks strewn about in the vast room, each covered in paperwork and coffee stains. Regular cops wore standard green outfits, detectives had on a shirt and tie, and Retrievers typically wore trench coats and hats. Standard cops tended to look down on the Retriever units, thinking our job too "easy" and unworthy of the badge. I always laughed at their attitudes. One day in our shoes and they'd be shitting themselves.

I glanced over at one of the primary screens that hung on the wall. It was about the only thing of technical significance in the main officers' area, other than our ancient computers and data pads. You'd think we'd have floating screens and such, but that kind of tech was reserved for people way above our pay grade.

I did a quick scan of the feeds for anything unusual. There were a couple of supernaturals who were due back within the next couple of days, but no one else was listed as overdue or missing.

"Okay, you two," Carter said with a grunt as he'd clearly finished up his thoughts, "get settled and then meet me in my office in an hour for a debriefing."

He then held me back as Reaper headed down the aisle toward what I presumed was his desk.

"How'd he do?"

"Well, he didn't have a gun, he jumped on an Empiric, and his eyes aren't exactly what you'd call stealth material."

Carter rubbed his chin. "Hmmm."

I couldn't completely throw Reaper under the bus here, though. The fact was that he *had* effectively saved me from the fun of getting pummeled with Death Nails.

"To be fair," I admitted with some effort, "he did put a normal in stasis before she died. He also got a shield around me before the vampires riddled my flesh with bullets."

"That's good," Carter replied after a moment. "So you think he'll work out as your new partner, then. Excellent."

I blinked a few times as he started walking away.

"I never said that, Chief," I called out after him. "He's got a lot to learn and you know I'm not fond of babysitting."

"You'll do your best, I'm sure."

As he turned into his office, I couldn't help but wish I'd thrown Reaper under the bus.

"Damn it."

I moved down the center aisle that separated the large space, headed for my station.

All desks were out in the open, lined up in rows, with no privacy whatsoever. It meant everyone was always in everyone else's business.

"What's the matter, Piper," teased Officer Brazen, one of the bigger assholes on the squad, "couldn't catch a simple vampire?"

He was big, out of shape, had a greasy beard, and his shirts were always spotted with some form of gravy or another. Seeing that he was a werebear, it made sense that he'd be somewhat sloppy, but there *was* such a thing as a dry cleaner.

I rolled my eyes. "Yeah, yeah, yeah."

Brazen's partner, Officer Kix, a younger djinn with a lean face and green eyes, leaned forward to reveal his shit-eating grin.

"Kind of hard to miss them," he chuckled, "seeing as they've got big fangs, you know?"

I leaned down, inches from his face. "Kind of hard to miss you, too, Kix, seeing that you're such a gigantic prick."

"Oooh," Brazen laughed. "Watch out, Kix, that girl might be more dangerous than she looks."

"Oh, Brazen," I said, pushing myself back up and holding my chest, "if you were only half the man your mother was."

"Fuck you, Piper."

"Thanks for the offer, but I prefer the company of the opposite sex."

Brazen leaned back in his chair and clasped his hands behind his head. "I've got something here that'll prove I'm all man."

"Great," I said with mock enthusiasm, "just let me go get my electron microscope and we'll have a look."

That shut him up.

I finally got to my desk and dropped off my coat before continuing down the hall to the elevators. I wanted to get with Dr. Hale to check on the status of the normal that Reaper had sent down earlier. After that, I'd pay Pecker a visit regarding those runes I'd seen.

Just as the elevator door was closing, a hand reached in and stopped it.

It was Reaper.

"Mind if I join you?" he asked, stepping inside and not waiting for an answer.

"Sure, why not?"

The elevator hit the lower level and then we stepped out and hit the doctor's office, expecting to see the normal being worked on.

Instead we found an empty unit.

"Hello, Piper," Dr. Hale said, coming up behind us. "Ah, good to see you, Reaper."

"And you as well," Reaper replied with a bow.

Dr. Hale was a middle-aged vampire who wore round-rimmed glasses that made her look studious. She was the grumpy type, too. We got along perfectly.

"Where is the normal?" I asked.

"She's been reversed," answered Hale while pointing back out the way we came, "but it wasn't easy. I have the crew modifying her memories right now and then we'll send her back. She'll just think she was drinking too much and passed out."

"What if she doesn't drink?" I asked.

"Hmmm. Good point." She shrugged. "Oh well, she does now."

"Right."

"Follow me for a second," Dr. Hale instructed, turning and walking toward a small room off in the corner. "I've got some questions."

We followed her and sat in the two chairs in front of her desk.

Dr. Hale sat down and clicked a few keys on her keyboard, causing her computer to come to life. She turned it around so it was facing us.

"This is the normal you sent me," Dr. Hale said, staring at the screen. "Notice anything strange?"

"You mean besides the fact that she's lying there like she's just been bitten by a vampire?"

"Yes," the answer was tight.

I looked at the picture more carefully. Everything seemed in order as far as I could tell. She had dark hair, a beige blouse, white skin, two little holes in her neck, black eyes, red nails, a gray skirt with—

"Black eyes," I said with a jolt. "Why does she have black eyes?"

I'd seen many a normal get bitten by a vampire over my years and never once did they end up having black eyes. We're not just talking the irises here, either. The *entire* eye was black.

"Her DNA had been altered beyond what vampires typically manage." She tilted her head at me. "Did the others seem like average vampires?"

"Best I can tell, they were," I answered and then glanced over at Reaper. "Reap?"

"I saw nothing unusual aside from the fact that they were carrying illegal weaponry and had runes assisting them."

"Yeah," I agreed. "There was that."

"So a wizard was helping them," Dr. Hale more stated

than asked. "That could have something to do with it, I suppose."

"What do you mean, Doc?"

"Just that whoever bit her had something more to them than simple vampirism," Dr. Hale said, tapping on the image of the normal on her screen. "I don't know what, exactly, but it sure as hell isn't just a vampire."

CHAPTER 7

*W*e took the elevator down another level and entered Pecker's workshop. Where Dr. Hale's place of work was clean and crisp, Pecker's was a complete wreck. How the little goblin could find his way around in all this mess was a mystery.

"This place is just as filthy as the last time I was here," jeered Reaper while holding up a hand to cover his mouth.

"Afraid you're going to catch something deadly, Reap?" I asked as we padded across the sticky floor. "I wouldn't have thought your kind could get sick."

He lowered his hand but said nothing.

"Pecker?" I called out after a few moments of waiting. "Are you in here?"

"Yeah, yeah," replied his heavily accented voice. "I'm comin' already. Hold your panties."

Okay, I wasn't fond of that comment, but for whatever reason, I never held a grudge against him. Maybe it was because he was a goblin or maybe it was because he had given me more tech over the years than anyone else I knew, but he got away with a lot more than I was known to tolerate.

Papers were flying in the air, signaling the path the little guy was taking to get to us.

Finally, he burst through a set of boxes and looked up at me. He had a narrow, gray face that was littered with wrinkles and creases. His ears were long and pointed, and they had hair poking out of their holes. He wiped his nose on his dirty lab coat.

"Piper," he said with a sigh, "what can I do ya for?" Then he paused and glanced at my new partner. "How's the tat, Reaper?"

"It's going very well, thank you," he replied.

"It needs ice storms and lightning bolts added," I interjected, thinking that if I was going to be saddled with this guy for the long haul, he needed some better firepower. "Also, if you can figure out a way to dim his high beams, that'd be great."

"Tough broad" said Pecker as he leaned in toward Reaper. "Gotta love her."

Reaper leaned back toward Pecker. "Must I?"

Great, so Reaper and Pecker were pals. He was probably also buddying up with Brazen and Kix. That'd have to stop.

"Actually," Pecker said, holding up a finger, "I could probably add in an energy matrix. That'd give you some extra power." He looked away for a few seconds while mumbling to himself. "Yeah, that should work."

He pushed away some papers from a keyboard and started typing wildly. The speed of his fingers was insane.

"You should write books," I suggested in awe. "You could release one a week at the speed you type."

"Nah," he said over his shoulder. "I'd drive reader teams insane if I did something like that!"

"Good point."

Reaper was looking at his tattoo as Pecker continued his changes. It was an interesting light show as little glowing wisps moved around.

"Can you feel that?" I asked.

"It tingles a little bit," Reaper answered.

A new line was beginning to form. This was the way tattoos were put on officers. You'd think we'd go through the old ink-and-needle method, but this was done through some means that tied magic and technology together.

"Annnnnnd done," announced Pecker with a final slam of the keyboard. He turned back. "You'd just use three fingers there and—" He slapped Reaper's hand away. "Not in here!"

"Oh, sorry."

Pecker wiped his forehead and let out a relieved breath.

"Right, well, it'll launch an energy pulse. You might want to be careful with it, though, because you're pretty different than everyone else." Pecker smiled. "It might be a big boom."

A big boom would have been nice when we were facing down those vampires. Granted, they used a Shredder to cause their own big boom, but we could have used a preemptive strike.

"Anyway," I said, "we were just topside dealing with a bunch of vampires and—"

"Assholes."

"What?"

"Vampires," he spat. "Most of them are assholes. Of course, so are werewolves and fae and pixies,"—he looked up at me again—"*especially* pixies, and djinn and mages and—"

"I get it," I interrupted. "Everyone but goblins are assholes."

"Oh, no, sister, we're the worst." He cracked a creepy smile at that. "Anyway, what about the vampires?"

"They had runes and I need to figure out if we can trace the mage or wizard who created them."

"Sure," he said, looking me over. "Are they in your pocket or something?"

I grimaced at him. I considered myself a pretty patient person, though I'm sure many now-deceased perps would disagree with that self-assessment, but sometimes I just wasn't in the mood to play around.

But he had a point. I should have just broken the wall and carried them back with me. It's not like the runes were that large, after all.

"I don't," I stated after a moment. "They were in a building that was burning down and the local fire department had just arrived."

"We could probably have gotten them, if we—" Reaper started.

"Then why didn't you?" I snarled at him before he could finish his sentence.

"Because I couldn't see them, Piper."

His reply was smooth and even.

It made my eye twitch.

"All I have is the memory of the damn things," I said, turning back to face Pecker. "Is there anything we can do from that?"

"That depends on how solid your memory is," he answered with a shrug. "Oh, and I'd also need you to recreate the magical signature exactly."

"Seriously?" I scoffed. "There's not some system that has a bunch of runes collected over the years that we can use as a comparison?"

"Sure there is," Pecker replied with an arched eyebrow, "but it doesn't work just from drawings."

I wanted to jump into a long diatribe about how that made no sense. Hell, there were even handwriting experts in the Overworld who could figure out the identity of a person just by their scribbles. But Pecker wasn't the type who responded well to having things like that pointed out to him. He'd just grumble something in response and I'd be on his shit list for a week.

Fortunately, there *was* a way to handle him that worked with nearly all engineers.

"I guess that makes sense," I said coyly. "It'd be great if there were some way to detect them by their specific painting styles."

"Hmmm," he said, eying me dubiously.

I had to play it carefully or he'd catch on.

"You mean like handwriting specialists do?" Reaper asked.

"Huh?" I answered in mock surprise. "I hadn't thought of that, actually." Then I gazed down at Pecker. "Maybe

41

that's out of your area of expertise, though? I mean, you're an engineer, not a—"

"I know what I am," he sassed while giving me the evil eye. "And I know what you are, too, Piper. You're a lousy, two-bit con artist who's trying to get me to build a system that will run comparisons on runes based solely on whose hand built it."

I batted my eyelashes at him. No, I wasn't one of those who went in for using my feminine wiles, but now and then they came in handy.

"Bitch," he said with a wink. "All right, all right. I'll give you that it's a decent enough idea, and I probably should have thought about it a long time ago, but there's not much call for rune-checking these days."

I smiled.

"Before you go getting all proud," he continued, "it's going to take some time to build this up, and it ain't going to work on you sketching your recollection of it." He wiped his nose again. "Your painting would have to be *exactly* like the wizard or mage who made that rune." He stared into my eyes firmly. "*Exactly*, Piper."

I sighed.

"Right."

"Next time bring me the board it's on and I'll see what I can do."

"Fair enough," I conceded with a groan, knowing the rune would have undoubtedly been destroyed by now, but maybe not. "I doubt it's still there at this point, but might be worth a look."

Pecker twitched his nose. "Sorry."

"Can't be helped," I replied. "Let's go, Reap. We've got some sleuthing to do."

We said our goodbyes and jumped back in the elevator. Chief Carter wanted answers; unfortunately, we had none.

"Don't you just love Pecker?" Reaper said, all smiles.

I frowned at him. "Really might want to think through your phrasing *before* you speak, Reap."

CHAPTER 8

*C*arter was just hanging up his phone when Reaper and I walked into his office.

"Okay," he said, "what do we know?"

"Not much more, Chief," I answered. "Dr. Hale found something weird with the normal that Reap sent down, but she's not exactly sure what's going on there."

Carter just kept his eyes on me as if waiting for more.

"Right," I continued, "we also met with Pecker to see if he could help us figure out who drew the runes."

"And?"

"No dice. Says he'd need the physical copies in order to do it, but he's also going to work on a way to piece it out just from images."

"Wonderful," Carter said as he rubbed his temples. "So we've got Gallien Cross running around town feeding, he's got help, and he's turning normals into something that our talented Dr. Hale doesn't understand."

I nodded. "That's about the gist of it, yep."

The room fell silent for a few minutes. Obviously the

chief was thinking things through, as was I, but at least he wasn't going off on a tangent regarding the fact that we didn't have enough information. He sometimes did just that when he was fuming. Right now, he looked more concerned than angry.

As far as chiefs went, Carter had always been a good one. He'd get irritated from time to time, and he could be quite pushy when necessary, but for the most part he was fair and decent. In fact, were it not for him, I'd be in prison.

I wasn't exactly what you'd call a model citizen, after all.

Before you go judging me, though, walk a few miles in my shoes. I was born a normal, my parents were killed by some mage who didn't want them to testify against him, I was raised in the Netherworld due to my special abilities to see supernaturals, and I was somehow infused with immortality. Nobody had ever figured that one out, including me.

Anyway, getting bullied and shit on all my life made me "gritty," at least that's what Chief Carter said when he'd come to a holding cell I'd been in due to fighting. He asked me if I wanted to use my grit to work for the Paranormal Police Department. It was either that or spend time in jail.

Obviously, I took the job.

That was six years ago.

"We need to get Cross off the streets," the chief breathed.

"Well," I said, using that grit that got me this job in the first place, "if I didn't have to keep an eye on junior here, that'd certainly help." I then looked at Reaper. "No offense."

"Some taken."

"Fact is that he's not ready and I can't be worried about him the entire time."

"If I recall correctly," Reaper remarked, "I believe it was my shield that saved your life earlier, Piper."

"I wouldn't have died. I'm immortal, remember?"

"It still would have hurt a fair bit and you would have required time to heal." I went to reply, but he held up a hand. "Also, Dr. Hale would never have had the chance to see how that woman's eyes changed to black. And while we don't understand yet what the blackness of that woman's eyes signifies, it may be a clue that you would not have uncovered without me."

I hated being wrong, but I was wrong.

Regardless, the fact was that I would be able to stop Gallien Cross by myself a hell of a lot easier without Reaper being around. I wouldn't hesitate like I did with him there. His wellbeing held me up when it shouldn't have been an issue. Truth was that he was just as immortal as I was, but that doesn't matter when you're in the thick of it. You don't consider things like that. You just think that you have someone else to cover.

I worked best alone.

Alone.

"Chief—" I started emphatically.

"Reaper," he said, cutting me off, "would you please give us the room?"

That wasn't good. If Carter had been wearing a red

47

suit with a black belt and white trimmings, I would have thought I was being put on the "naughty list."

"Of course, Chief," Reaper said after a moment of staring at me.

Once he was out the door, I wanted to lay into Carter for putting me in this situation in the first place, but his face told me that now wasn't the time.

"Piper," he said with a sigh, "you're our best Retriever."

Wasn't expecting that.

Reverse psychology, maybe?

I'd have to keep my guard up.

"Okay," I said with a squint.

"I'm not playing any games here," he said, clearly catching my leery attitude. He motioned around at his paper-littered desk. "I've got twenty-seven Retrievers on staff, and most of them are very good at what they do. I've got over two hundred cops, too. Again, they're solid. I mean, sure, some need a little work…"

"Brazen and Kix."

"Among others," he affirmed. "But you're the only one I don't worry about. You go out, you get the job done, and you report back in. No fuss, no muss. All business."

"Thanks," I said, still thinking he was trying to set a hook.

"It's why I put you on the toughest cases," he continued. "It's also why I agreed to let you work alone after Officer Michaels left the force. You're a rebel. That makes you dangerous and effective, which is *precisely* what it takes to be a good Retriever."

There was no arguing that. I'd seen a few Retrievers

over the years who seemed to be a shoo-in for the job, but when the action went down, they couldn't handle it. It wasn't enough to be willing to shoot people, you also had to watch out for the normals. Yes, there was collateral damage from time to time, but you avoided it where you could.

My mind dropped back to Reaper jumping on the Empiric.

Shit.

"All right, Chief," I said finally, "what's your point?"

His eyes locked in on mine. "That I need my best officer to help improve my other officers."

"What? I'm not a fucking teacher!"

"Watch your language in here, young lady," he said hotly.

"Sorry, Chief." I knew he hated it when I went all potty-mouth around him. "But we've got an escaped prisoner who is up in the Overworld feeding on normals and doing something fu...messed up to their DNA. Is this really the time for me to be playing sensei to some dude who has spent his entire existence waiting for people to die?"

Without hesitation, Carter said, "Yes."

"Why?"

"Because Gallien Cross is not just some basic escapee, Piper."

That stopped my angst.

"He's not?"

It was Carter's turn to look concerned.

"Didn't you read the full dossier on him?"

The chief had asked that question in a very accusatory

tone. I wasn't fond of that one because it usually meant I'd done something wrong.

"I might have missed a few things," I said, chewing my lip, "like everything after his face, name, the fact that he is a vampire, and that he likes feeding on normals." I threw up my hands when the chief shook his head at me. "What's the problem? He's a bad guy who escaped and needs to be brought back. I do this all the time. They comply or die. Simple. I don't care what they did or didn't do."

"So much for you being my best Retriever," Carter said with a sigh as he threw a file at me. Carter was still the type who preferred paper to digital. "Read it."

I opened the doc and read the summary.

Gallien Cross is a vampire who was imprisoned for feeding on normals. He was captured in 1982 and sentenced to 50 years in prison without parole. He was also slated to go through deep reintegration every year until his date of release.

"Yeah," I said, holding out the folder, "I've read this already."

"Go to the next page, Officer Shaw," Carter said, using my title.

I hated it when he did that.

Cross was most widely known for working with mages and wizards to infuse vampirism with magic and the blood of the normal. This caused normals to become vampires who were easily controlled by him. His goal was to create an army of them. The tell-tale sign of an infused normal is their black eyes. The practice came to be known as the Blood Crossed Rituals.

I'd heard the stories about this, of course. It was in the Retriever training program and everything. In my defense, it wasn't like the name "Gallien" was unique in the Netherworld, and there had been a Gallien Cross who held political office at one point, too. Different guy, but that was in the nineties, so he was more recent.

"Oh," I said, feeling sheepish, "that was this guy?"

"Obviously," Carter said, snatching the file from my hands. "Maybe I *should* stick Reaper with someone else."

There was a light at the end of the tunnel.

"Agreed, Chief," I said, looking as downtrodden as I could manage. "I'm not worthy to be anyone's teacher." I groaned for effect. "The shame of it all."

"Nice try, smart-butt," he said. Again, he wasn't one to use foul language. "Unfortunately, for you, I know you'll learn from this, which I can't say about a lot of people."

"I probably won't," I chimed in. "Honestly, Chief, I just can't be trusted."

"Seeing that you *will* learn from this," he continued with that same level of grit I'd been cursed with, "I'm going to make things even more interesting for you."

I didn't like the sound of that.

"We've got a couple of officers who have been wanting to get into the RTP lately."

The RTP was the Retriever Training Program. It's where every officer had to go in order to get into the Retrievers. Graduates were few and far between, which made me wonder why Reaper had made it through. He wasn't exactly the best candidate I'd ever seen. My only guess was that his unique perspective on life, or death, was deemed useful.

"You're worrying me, Chief," I said, noting the twinkle in his eye.

JOHN P. LOGSDON & CHRISTOPHER P. YOUNG

The twinkle stopped.

He just wasn't great at being a disciplinarian.

"Look, Piper," he said, putting his elbows on the desk, "I know you want to go after this guy alone, and I honestly thought you'd have a chance when I assigned you this case, but—"

"I could have had him if it weren't for Reaper, Chief. He caused me to hesitate. I can't do this job if I'm hesitating."

"So you said," he replied. "Fact is, though, that you also said Cross has a suite of goons and he's been feeding, and the normals he's feeding on all have that blackened eyes thing that stuck Cross in prison in the first place."

"Right?"

"You need backup, Piper."

The three most dreaded words in my time as a Retriever were "You need backup." I didn't *want* backup. I wanted to sneak around, slide up behind a perp, knock his ass out and drag him home, or shoot him and drag what was left of him home.

Backup sucked.

I couldn't do stealthy with backup.

"Oh, come on, Chief," I whined. "So I didn't read the full dossier. I *never* read the full dossier." Okay, probably not something I should have said. "But I will going forward. You've got my word."

"That's not why I'm doing this, Piper," he replied. Then he bobbed his head around slightly. "Okay, it's partially why I'm doing this. But the real reason is that you need backup and that makes this the perfect scenario."

"Sticking me in a teaching role while dealing with a very dangerous perp is the perfect scenario?" I countered.

That made very little sense to me.

"Yes." Again, no hesitation.

"How?"

"Because I have two cops who want to be Retrievers, and you know quite well that seasoned officers must go through a very trying experience in the field before they can even be considered for the RTP."

No arguing that. Standard cops were used to a certain way of working. They needed to be thrown directly into the shit of what Retrievers underwent so they could see exactly what they were up against.

"What if they get killed?" I said.

"Then they weren't cut out for the RTP program," he said sadly. "You know the deal."

I wanted to gripe some more, but there was no point. Carter's mind was made up.

Time to get stoic.

"They'll be fully under my command?"

"Absolutely," he answered. "I'll make doubly sure they understand that."

I leaned my head back and looked up at the ceiling.

"Fine," I said after taking a deep, cleansing breath. "Who is it?"

"Brazen and Kix."

I snapped my head forward.

"You're fucking kidding me."

"Language!"

CHAPTER 9

I headed back to my desk with the chief in tow. Brazen and Kix had their heads down, working on something, and Reaper was messing around with his tattoo.

"Don't launch any energy pulses in here," I warned him.

He didn't bother to dignify my comment with a remark.

The chief gave me an apologetic glance and sighed. He knew how I felt about this, but we all had our jobs to do, so I rolled my eyes and motioned for him to go for it.

"Officers Brazen and Kix," he said, jolting them from their paperwork, "you're going to be working with Piper and Reaper in a supporting role."

Brazen's face creased at the sound of that.

"A supporting role?" he quavered in disbelief. "To Piper?"

"Well, at least your hearing works, Officer Brazen," the

JOHN P. LOGSDON & CHRISTOPHER P. YOUNG

chief said. "That's good. It'll help when you formally apply to the RTP, assuming Piper vouches for you, of course."

"I...what?"

Kix could only blink in response.

Okay, so it was kind of fun to watch both of these bozos squirm under the realization that *I* held their futures in my hands.

Oh, the power.

"Comprehension isn't great," stated the chief with a grin. "You might want to improve that." He smiled at me. "Bottom line is that you two are going to be under Piper's command, alongside Reaper here, until I say so. Is that clear?"

They both nodded painfully.

"Good. If she passes you, I'll put in a recommendation to the brass to get you both in the Retriever Training Program; if she fails you, you've got another year to wait." He leaned in and looked at them both. "I'd recommend you not aggravate her, gentlemen."

This was getting better and better.

"Piper," the chief announced, "they're all yours."

With that, he headed back to his office, leaving me standing there with one glowing-eyed partner and two dumbass apprentices.

Super.

"All right," I said, taking immediate control of the situation, "here's the deal: Reaper and I are going to go topside to the warehouse we were at earlier, in the hopes that those runes are still intact." I glanced at Reaper. "My guess is they're not."

"Not likely," he agreed.

"You two," I continued, pointing at Brazen and Kix, "are going to scour every piece of information from every intel portal you can to see if you can spot anything that leads us to Gallien Cross. You'll find his file online. Read the *entire* thing. Got it?"

"Whatever you say, *boss*," Brazen snarked.

I chose to ignore his sass. It wasn't easy.

"My gut tells me that he's not going to be all that easy to track because he has goons that we couldn't see."

"So?" asked Kix, frowning.

"So we caught up to him pretty soon after his escape," I clarified. "By now he may be employing the same methods that the goons were in order to avoid detection."

"Ah, gotcha."

Of the two, Kix was definitely less of a pain in the ass. He was still annoying, no doubt, but I had a feeling he'd handle his new role easier than Brazen would.

"Any questions?" I asked. There were none. "Good. We'll be back in thirty minutes, tops. Anything you two can find to help us plan our next move would be nice."

"Yeah, yeah," said Brazen. "We're on it."

Even with his future in my hands, he was still a nutsack.

I headed off toward the portal, not bothering to look back.

"Let's go, Reap."

CHAPTER 10

*T*he warehouse was still dripping and there were a number of firetrucks around.

We'd set the portal to deliver us up the street, away from the warehouse. This way we wouldn't risk being spotted by anyone who may be lingering at the scene.

Unlike the standard PPD officers, we were able to jump to non-portal sites. We also arrived within a null zone and a hidden zone. This made it easier on us to sneak up on supers who could see into null zones, while not freaking out the normals who couldn't see into either the null or hidden zones.

"Looks like there's still a lot going on down there," Reaper said.

I smirked. "Well, at least your sleuthing chops are top-notch, Reap. Can you lower your headlights?"

"Sorry."

"Can everyone see those lamps or just supers?"

Last thing we needed was some normal spotting the glowing Mr. Payne. That would send up a shit storm in

JOHN P. LOGSDON & CHRISTOPHER P. YOUNG

the local papers. Nobody would believe the guy, but Reaper and I would end up getting grilled by the Netherworld Sensitivity Council, which was never fun. I knew this for a fact because I was pretty sure my number was one of their speed-dial options.

"Normals can't see them," he replied.

"Well, that's good, at least."

We began our walk down toward the warehouse, keeping to the side of the road and out of sight. There was no point in raising suspicion from anyone down there.

"Why do they get brighter anyway?" I asked as we crept past a car. "You have problems seeing in the dark?"

"I can see fine in the dark," he answered. "My eyes glow because of my energy. The more amped up I am, the brighter my eyes get. Think of it like your heartbeat. When you're excited, your pulse races."

"But you can dim them pretty fast."

"Yes," he answered. "Doing so doesn't diminish my state of arousal. It's just one more thing I have to focus on if asked."

I understood that. Still, those flashy things were going to get us in trouble if he didn't do something about them.

"Another thing they do is allow me to erase any person's memory."

I stopped and looked at him.

Had he just said what I thought he said?

"Once again?" I said, blinking.

"Reapers sometimes arrive on a scene to find a person very close to death," he explained. "We don't always know if they will survive or not. But in the moments where they hover between the two realities, they can see us. If the person survives, we must erase this memory."

That was some useful information to know.

"You mean like that flashy thingy they used in the movie *Men in Black*?"

"I have no point of reference, I'm afraid," he said, pondering, "but I can say that we are disallowed from using this power except in the most extreme of circumstances."

Also good to know. Reaper didn't seem like the kind of guy who would abuse that power, but it was obvious he did do *something* to warrant being kicked out of the reaper community for a while. That meant he wasn't Mr. Goody Two-Shoes either.

I started walking down again until we got to the back of the warehouse.

The entire back wall had been demolished and the area where the runes had been was gone, too.

"Damn it."

"Indeed," agreed Reaper. "Hopefully our new partners will have found some information we can use."

"Ew," I said, throwing up a little in my mouth. "Don't call them that."

I went to transport back, when I saw a face off in the distance. It was almost invisible the way it was hidden in the shadows, but I was damn certain that it was a face.

"Wait," I said to Reaper before he could finish his transport sequence. "Don't look now, but to my right there is someone standing in the shadows."

He looked.

I put my hands on my hips. "You're really not good at following instructions, are you?"

"Sorry."

"There's no doubt your glowing orbs were noticed just then, so this may be moot, but do you have any ability to track people at all?" I was struggling to keep my cool "Or is everything in your arsenal of usefulness contained in that tattoo of yours?"

In response, he closed his eyes and began moving his head around. It was as if he were studying the area in some way that didn't require vision. Either that, or his vision didn't rely on his eyes.

He stopped.

"There are three people in the direction you indicated," he said calmly. "They are all radiating the same feeling that I got from the woman I delivered to Dr. Hale earlier, but these three are all male."

"Can you pinpoint them exactly?"

His nod was almost imperceptible.

That gave me an idea.

"Okay," I said, turning and walking away from where the three were hiding out, "let's head up here, turn a corner, and then transport to where they're located. Once we show up, I'll drop them, you put them in stasis, and we send Dr. Hale another gift."

He looked like he was about to argue with me, or at least question my methods, but he held himself in check.

"Sync your tattoo with mine," he said finally, "and I will control the transport."

Now we were getting somewhere.

CHAPTER 11

*W*e blinked into existence about ten feet behind our prey.

"Turn off your fucking eyes, Reap," I yelled through the connector.

"Sorry," he replied aloud.

"Oh, for fuck's sake," I answered as the three men spun and glared at us. Well, I assumed they were glaring. It was hard to tell with their eyes being black and us being in a mostly dark area. "Honest to shit, Reap, you're going to have to fix that problem and get your connector right or I'll kick your ass from here all the way back to reaper land."

"I shall get some shades," he mumbled. Then, he brightened and said, "Would you like me to send an energy pulse at them?"

It was an option, and so was a shield.

But these guys didn't have any weapons that I could see, so my guess was that they were bitten and left for dead. Either that or they were placed here to keep an eye on any Retrievers who came back to the scene.

The three began to growl.

"Step back, Reap," I commanded. "My plan is to kick the shit out of these three and then you'll put them in stasis. Got it?"

"As you say," he stated before moving back.

This was not one of those fights where I wanted to use a gun. My hope was a couple of quick kicks and a punch here and there would be all it would take to subdue these three. They didn't look all that dangerous, from what I could tell.

As if to challenge my thoughts, the one on the left hissed and launched at me faster than should have been possible.

I rolled with the swipe of his hands, noting the razor-sharp claws that stuck an inch out from his fingers. Fortunately they only grazed my cheek, because that would have sucked.

Continuing my spinning motion, I swung an elbow around and clipped him on the back of his head, driving him headfirst into the wall of the brick building we were standing beside. There was an unfortunate thud that went along with the collision. My gut said he wasn't going to wake up from it.

The remaining two hissed and jumped at me in unison.

That was bullshit. Hadn't they ever seen any kung fu movies? Whenever multiple people attacked, it was supposed to be done one at a time. It was only fair.

But I was ready for their speed this time.

I dived forward, under their arc. Then I rolled and sprang back to my feet, spinning back to face them in one smooth motion. My left hand was up and my left leg was forward. I was ready to kick or punch or whatever.

At least their tell was obvious.

Another hiss and a dive, right at my face. Apparently they didn't get the memo regarding body shots being quite effective.

This time I grabbed the guy's wrist and spun around, bringing his inertia to full bore against him. He was flying when I spun back and twisted his arm with enough force that he flipped over. Typically this move looks great on paper but doesn't do much in the wild, but I had a feeling it'd work because these dudes were all-in on their attacks, giving me leverage.

I snapped a kick to the side of his head and he passed out.

Two down, one to go.

Just as the last one was about to hiss, Reaper stepped up and karate-chopped him on the neck.

"Nice," I said as the body hit the ground, but I felt a little disappointed.

Reaper shook his head at me. "I thought we may wish to have at least one of them still breathing."

That sounded like an admonishment. Who was he to talk to me like that? If it weren't for him and his glowing eyes and loud mouth, I could have knocked these three out quietly.

Besides, I'd only killed one of them.

"He's alive," I argued, pointing at the guy I'd just dropped.

"He's truly not," Reaper disagreed while putting his quarry in stasis. "His head hit a rock when you flipped him over. Your kick only made a bad situation worse."

I knelt down and checked the dude's pulse.

Nothing.

That was odd. These were vampires, right? They had the fangs and the nails, but they couldn't take a punch?

"Oh, well, shit." Then I glanced over at Reaper. "Wait a second here. How'd you know he was dead, Reap?"

"I felt it."

Yet another useful piece of the puzzle that was Reaper Payne.

"Right." I stood up and brushed off my clothes. "Well, send that guy back and let's get to the station and see if Brazen and Kix have found anything useful."

"That's what I'm doing," he affirmed with an edge.

I turned and stared down at him as he expertly ran his fingers over his tattoo. Obviously he was good at using that thing, but it didn't mean he knew the life of a Retriever. Chances were he hadn't been put through that first-mission crap like Brazen and Kix were about to feel, but it was also clear that he wasn't one who would easily play second fiddle in this one-woman band.

"Something you want to say, Reap?" I challenged.

He didn't bother to look up. "Not really."

"Good."

CHAPTER 12

I'd decided it was best to send off all three bodies to Dr. Hale, even though two of them were dead. There was no sense in leaving them in the Overworld for someone to stumble upon, at least not without first clearing whatever Cross had done to them out of their systems. Besides, I wanted to know what exactly would allow them to have some of the vampire traits but not all. Obviously it had to do with the magical infusion, but I was hoping Hale could shed some light on it.

"What have you guys learned?" I asked Brazen and Kix as we got back to our desks. "Something useful, I hope?"

"We went through everything," Brazen stated as he pointed at his screen, "but there's just no tracking this guy."

"Wait," interjected Kix before I could say anything. "I've been scanning around for his past known acquaintances and I think I've got something."

He tapped on his keyboard for a couple of seconds and

then clicked his mouse to reveal one of the Netherworld's video feeds at The Ruby Slipper. He zoomed it around until he locked in on someone who looked a lot like Gallien Cross.

"That's him," I said, pointing. "I think."

"I concur," agreed Reaper. "Shall we go and—"

"No, wait," I said, holding him back. "Who is he seated with?"

"Checking."

Kix started typing again. He wasn't anywhere near the speed of Pecker, but it'd take a robot to match that goblin.

"Jax Mitchell," he said finally. "He's traceable."

"Any history?"

"Uh…" More typing. "He did some time in the nineties for robbery."

I nodded. "What did he steal?"

"Jewels and some cash."

"Looks like a shifter of some sort," Brazen spoke out, hovering over my shoulder. "Guessing wolf, but he's kind of small."

"Vampire," Kix stated after a few seconds.

"Why does this matter?" asked Reaper.

I started chewing my nails as I thought. Then I grunted at myself and stopped. I hated that habit and I'd been trying to stop it for quite some time, but it was a subconscious reaction that happened whenever my brain was faced with a puzzle.

"Helps to know what you're facing when you go in for a fight," answered Kix.

"Piper doesn't seem to care what race they are," Reaper stated. "Her killing is equal opportunity."

I furrowed my brow at him and sniffed.

Fact was, he was right. I couldn't give two shits if you were a djinn or a pixie, if you ran I was going to hunt you down. If I could bring you back alive, I got 100% of my commission; if you fought to get away, I'd happily take 25% commission and drag whatever remained of your carcass back as proof of a kill.

"How are these two connected?" I asked to the air.

"We can dig into that," offered Brazen, which was kind of a surprise. "Unless you want us to go with you topside?"

I gave him an appraising glance. Was he actually trying *not* to be an asshole? I wasn't sure I was fond of that prospect.

"No, you're right," I said, nearly reeling in shock that I had to say those words to him...ever. "Dig up what you can on this guy. Reap and I will go and see if we can grab hold of Gallien before he—"

"He's moving," Kix interrupted. "Sorry, Piper, but he's moving."

"Shit. Any cameras around that you can use to follow him?"

He started accessing things, but it was clear that this was over his head. Honestly, I was impressed he'd gotten as far as he had.

"Don't worry about it," I said, calming him down. "Go back to Jax. Is he still there?"

The video came back online.

"Yeah, he's there."

"Let's pay him a visit, Reap," I yelled as I started for the

JOHN P. LOGSDON & CHRISTOPHER P. YOUNG

portal. "You guys see what you can dig up on their relationship, if anything."

"You got it," Brazen called back.

Honestly, I wasn't fond of his compliancy at all.

It was making my skin crawl.

CHAPTER 13

We got to The Ruby Slipper just as our pal Jax was getting up to leave.

I was hoping there'd be a convenience store nearby so Reaper could get a pair of shades, but no such luck.

"Jax," I said, pushing him back into the booth, "we have a few questions, if you've got a minute?"

"Doesn't seem like I have much of a choice," he said, scooting over.

He was a small guy with straggly black hair, beady eyes, and a thin mustache. He was also very fidgety. I knew he'd just had an encounter with Gallien, which would put most people on edge, but this guy had "victim" written all over him.

"You were just talking with Gallien Cross," I stated. "He's an escaped prisoner from the Netherworld and it's my job to get him back."

"*Our* job," corrected Reaper.

I gave him a look.

"Retrievers, eh?" Jax whispered and then swallowed hard. "I...uh..."

"You're going to tell us what he told you," I pushed. "That way you don't end up going to jail also. It's pretty simple, actually."

He licked his lips and looked around as if trying to find a way to escape. We had him boxed in pretty well, though. He wasn't going anywhere.

Finally, his shoulders slumped.

"I can't tell you anything," he groaned. "If I do, he'll kill my wife."

"What?"

"Why would he kill your wife?" asked Reaper.

Jax gave him a serious look. "I literally just told you I can't tell you anything."

"You'd rather go to jail?" I asked.

I couldn't actually take him to prison for not giving us information, and it wasn't like he was harboring a fugitive. He could just as easily say that he had no idea where Gallien was staying and we couldn't prove otherwise.

But I had to try.

"I would," Jax answered soberly. "My wife is everything to me. I can't risk her life over this. If you take me to jail, Gallien will know I didn't talk." He then looked around with worry. "Actually, if you *don't* take me to jail he might think I *did* talk."

"That puts a wrinkle in things, doesn't it, Piper?" Reaper admonished.

Okay, so I hadn't considered the point before making the threat.

"We can't actually take you to jail for not telling us something, Jax," I revealed. "Sorry."

"Son of a bitch," he said with a scowl. "Thanks a lot, you fuckers."

"Don't worry," I said calmly. "If we walk out of here looking annoyed, he'll read that in our body language and know we've got nothing out of you."

"We'll have to make it abundantly obvious."

"I know, Reap." Then I reconsidered things. "You know, it wouldn't have mattered anyway seeing that we were going to talk to you one way or another, Jax."

He was seething at this point.

I guess I couldn't blame him. While I'd never had a serious significant other, I wasn't completely heartless. Even though Jax was clearly mixed up in a bad situation, it didn't mean his wife was at fault. She could have just been in the unfortunate circumstance of having fallen in love with the wrong guy.

It happens.

Me, I'm more into the concept of one-night stands. If I get horny, I find a dude who's looking for the same thing I am. No phone numbers, no flowers, no mushy shit. Just a hopefully-not-so-quick boom and done.

Relationships took more effort than I was willing to give.

Besides, it was the rare guy who would be cool with the fact that I was a Retriever. We had a reputation for being somewhat controlling and prone to violence. Some guys were cool with that. Ian Dex of the Las Vegas PPD came to mind. He was the best I'd had, in fact, which made sense considering what he was, but my limit with any partner was a single tryst. Anything beyond that moved into relationship territory.

Still, just because I wasn't into building a life with someone didn't mean I couldn't understand why someone like Jax would be freaking out at the moment.

"We'll make a show of it," I said. "Don't worry."

"Don't look now," Reaper said while keeping his mouth still, "but I think I see Haley across the street."

"The girl who was with Gunter and Philip at the docks?" I said as I immediately looked over.

Then I grimaced, as I knew what was coming.

"You're really not good at following instructions, are you?" Reaper asked, repeating verbatim what I'd said to him earlier that night.

"Damn it," I spat as Haley took off.

We jumped up from the booth and ran out of The Ruby Slipper.

I scanned the area and caught Haley running at full speed down Magazine Street.

"Can you track her, Reap?"

"I've got her."

His eyes were shut again.

"Can you run like that?"

"Yes."

I nodded and took off across the street and then tore down the sidewalk. She was fast, and she had a head start, but I was known to have some decent times on the forty-yard dash myself. Besides, with Reaper's crazy tracking thing going on, we'd catch her eventually.

"Out of the way," I was yelling. "Move it!"

"Fuck you," came one drunkard's response.

There was no time to pluck him in the balls so I just kept running.

Reaper didn't say a word. He just kept pace with me as I plowed ahead.

I could see Haley just fine from where I was until she cut around the corner past the building on the other side of Sixth Street.

From here it was up to Reaper to keep her in his sights.

We hit sixth and Reaper sped past me, proving he could really move when needed. He ran directly across toward the GNC nutrition store, and then turned right into a courtyard just past it.

Standing there waiting for us were Haley and a mass of goons.

We'd been set up.

CHAPTER 14

*T*his time I didn't even think twice. I just pulled out my gun and let all hell break loose.

Reaper threw up a shield and it was clear that Haley's crew hadn't done the same. I knew this because two of her crew ate Death Nails and were systematically ripped apart. There was a level of catharsis in that for me, being honest.

But then a bullet tagged me on the shoulder.

"Your shield is off, Reap," I yelled out as I hit the dirt while the pain radiated through my arm. "I just got hit."

"The shield isn't for us, Piper," he replied. "I'm trying to protect the normals. They're not immortals, if you may recall."

Smart ass.

I scurried over toward his position while firing. He didn't have to cover me, but if I got close enough to him, I'd be protected either way.

And, yes, I knew I was immortal, but getting shot still sucked. Smack your finger with a hammer. Probably won't kill you, but it'll still make you damn well wish you'd never smacked your finger with a hammer.

I'd be healed within thirty seconds anyway.

Haley was backing off as I fired at her. While her crew was open for business, she obviously had protection of her own because nothing was getting through.

And then something even worse happened.

"We've got a bunch of those things with the dark eyes incoming," I said to Reaper, and then realized that describing them like that wasn't going to be easy. "Let's call them ravens," I added.

"Why?"

"Because of their eyes, that's why."

"I don't get it."

He looked genuinely confused.

I pointed at the beasts.

"They look like ravens, Reap."

"They do?"

There was no time to debate the point or to bring up images of ravens and go through the details on why I thought it was a good name for them. I'd needed a name and I thought it fit.

"That's what I'm calling them," I stated before unleashing another round of Death Nails at the goons. "Deal with it."

"You're an odd person, Piper," Reaper replied.

"Says the guy with the glowing eyes."

Normals were gathering around the area, which was not good. They weren't likely seeing much, but it probably appeared odd.

Fortunately, I was able to counter this type of thing

pretty easily. I dropped to a knee, keeping within Reaper's shield, and hit a few lines on my tattoo.

Instant null zone.

And it had reach.

In a flash, all of the normals scattered like roaches when you flip on a light.

"Good thinking," Reaper said. "I can focus on protecting us now."

The ravens were coming at us like a bunch of...well, ravens. They were fast and there was no way I could shoot them all. I also doubted they'd honor that one-at-a-time fighting ritual.

"Fuck the shield," I cried as I dropped one magazine and expertly loaded another. "Shoot these bastards."

"You mean I can use the energy bolt?"

"I don't give a shit what you use, just do it!"

Three seconds later I regretted making that statement.

A plume of energy rolled across my body with such force that it felt like I was being torn apart at a molecular level. It hurt like nothing I'd ever experienced before. The pain was incredible.

Screams radiated from the goons, and the ravens too, telling me that they were experiencing the same level of joy I was. But where I was still managing to stay conscious, the bad guys were literally disintegrating.

Honestly, I felt a bit envious of them at that moment.

Once the area was clear, Reaper fell down on his face and groaned.

I tried to ask if he was okay, but my mouth wouldn't work, so I used the connector. Even that required a fair bit of effort.

"*Reap?*" I said, barely able to think straight.

"*I'm completely drained,*" he replied, using the connector this time.

My eyes felt like sandy marbles, but I managed to glance around the area. It was empty. Reaper's energy blast had obliterated all the supers and ravens. The memory of them being ripped apart would haunt my dreams for some time to come.

"*You did good,*" I said.

"*Well,*" he replied.

"*Well what?*"

"*The proper language is to say 'you did well,' not 'you did good.'*"

I snorted. "*You're a dick, Reap.*"

"*Thanks.*"

We lay there for a couple of minutes while allowing our bodies to heal and our strength to return.

Finally I pushed myself up and then helped Reaper to his feet.

"I'm guessing this is what having a migraine headache feels like," he moaned while holding his head. "I can't say I recommend it."

"I think your energy pulse thingy needs some fine-tuning," I commented while shutting down the null zone. "If nothing else, it'd be great if *I* wasn't impacted by it."

"And if it didn't sap all *my* energy," he added.

Normals started walking down the street again once the zone was lifted. They were oblivious to what had just taken place here. To them, there were just a couple of people standing in the courtyard next to the GNC.

"There's another rune over there," I said, pointing to a

board that was propped against the side wall near the back of the courtyard. "Let's bring it with us this time."

Just as we started toward it, Haley reappeared, smiled, launched *two* Empirics at us, and then disappeared again.

Reap immediately dived on his.

He looked up at me, back at the normals who were walking past, back at me again, and then down at the other Empiric.

"Aw, fuck," I said as I jumped on top of the damn thing.

CHAPTER 15

"What the hell happened to you guys?" asked Pecker as he studied our decimated jackets and ripped shirts. "Not that I mind the look on you, Piper."

"What?" I replied sourly.

"Hey, just because I'm a goblin doesn't mean I'm against playing a game of hide-the-little-goblin with a human."

"That's probably the grossest thing I've ever heard," I revealed, "and I've heard some pretty gross shit."

He looked injured by my comment.

Too bad.

This was the workplace and statements like his were not appropriate here. If I played nice about it, I'd end up getting dick pics from him within a week. Goblin dick-pics may press the right buttons for some people, but I wasn't one of them. Not that I'd ever seen a goblin dick before. For all I knew, they were the same as...

I shook myself.

Why was I thinking about this at all?

"Look," I said, trying to keep from wincing, "I snagged this rune from where we were just battling."

He took it from me.

"What kind is it?"

"Shield," I answered. "Just like the last one, but this is only meant for a single person."

He nodded and gave it the once-over.

"Can you actually see it?" I asked with surprise.

"Not at all," he answered, turning the board around and studying it. "I'm just not sure if it will fit in the machine." He glanced up at me. "Is the rune covering the entire board or can we cut it down farther?"

"Covers the entire thing."

"Crud," he said with a grunt. "Okay, we'll give it a shot anyway."

He kicked boxes and threw papers out of the way as he headed to another machine.

It was a blocky box that looked kind of like a microwave oven, but bigger. There were knobs and buttons that sat above a little glass window. Pecker opened it and worked to shove the rune board inside. It looked like it wasn't going to make it, but with a little finagling he was finally able to get it set.

Once in place, he closed up the machine and pressed a button.

Then he walked back to us.

"It'll take a couple of hours," he announced. "Hopefully I'll have something for you in the morning."

"Why so long?"

"There's a lot to these things, Piper," he replied while

crossing his arms. "It has to trace the rune perfectly, read in the color nuances and shading, and then do a rune-by-rune comparison with every item in our database. Once it collects runes that are close, it repeats the process against those to compare magical signatures."

"Ah."

"Don't worry," he said, wiping his hands together, "I'll hit you up as soon as I know something."

So much for walking in and getting a quick answer.

I supposed it was only fair that his system be given time to run through its checks in order to get the most accurate reading, but the longer this rune maker was out there, the more chances Gallien and his crew had to cause havoc in New Orleans.

"Hey, Pecker," Reaper said after a moment, "any chance you can make some tweaks to this energy pulse thing you gave me?"

"What's wrong with it?"

"Nothing's wrong with it," Reaper replied quickly, "it's just that—"

"It knocked the shit out of everyone in the area," I interrupted, "including me, and it drained Reap of almost all his energy."

"Huh." Pecker started up his typing again. "Did you focus it?"

"I don't know how."

"Oh, well, that'd do it…wait."

He was scanning over a bunch of gibberish on his screen. I knew it was computer code of some sort, but I couldn't understand a lick of it. Based on the fact that Reaper's face was scrunched up so tight that he looked like he'd had one too many tacos, I assumed he couldn't understand it either.

"Damn," said the little goblin. "I didn't integrate this properly. One sec."

His fingers took off again and so did the little lines on Reaper's arm. This time I noticed my new partner was not quite enjoying the changes being made. My guess was that this had to do with the lines being *undrawn* and then redrawn. I'd never seen lines get taken off a tattoo before.

"Okay, that should do it." Pecker walked over and pointed at the new lines. "These two will allow you to control the field of fire." He moved his finger to another tendril. "That one is for setting the power, and that one fires it."

"Got it," said Reaper.

"Sorry about the mixup," Pecker said with a slight bow. "I also fixed the wiring matrix so you don't get such a power drain. It'll still eat your energy—that can't be helped. But hopefully it won't be nearly as bad."

Reaper nodded. "Thanks, Pecker. You're the best."

"I do what I can," the goblin replied with a wave of his hand.

"Right," I said before this bout of man-love could continue. "We've got work to do. Let me know when you get a bead on the mage who made that rune, Pecker."

"You got it, hot stuff."

I turned back to him with menace in my eyes. He put up his hands in surrender.

"Sorry! Sheesh!"

CHAPTER 16

*D*r. Hale had a body on the table as we walked in. It was one of the ravens, though he appeared to be in transition back to normal.

I'd called Brazen and Kix down to join us so they could be part of the process. They'd been to Hale's office plenty of times over the years, no doubt, but they'd never seen anything like this. If they were going to get the full experience of being a Retriever, they needed to be here.

"I have some info, Doc," I said as she was hovering over the body. "These guys aren't fully turned vampires."

"Yes, I know."

"Right, but they are built for attacking only."

She paused what she was doing and looked at me. "Yes, I know."

"Oh."

"When this last batch came in, I pulled up your records to see who it was you were chasing," she explained. "Then I dug into his past and found out about the rituals. From there, I scoured the records of the previous two doctors who were around when Gallien Cross was doing his deeds."

That put a nail in that discussion. Frankly, she probably knew more about it than I did at this point.

"Could you maybe let us in on things?" asked Brazen.

I pointed at the body. "That's a raven—"

"A raven?" asked Dr. Hale. "I didn't see anything about that in the records."

"That's just what Piper has chosen to call these creatures, Doctor," Reaper stated. "I don't quite understand it either."

"Oh, come on," I badgered him. "It's really not that hard. Have you ever seen a raven?"

"The bird?" asked Kix.

"No," I snarked, "the football team. Yes, I'm talking about the bird."

All of them nodded.

"Well, look at that guy's face."

They did, and that should have been all it took to prove my point. Unfortunately, the dude was in the midst of changing back.

"Okay, not him," I said with a shrug, "but what he looked like before the doc got to work on him."

"We've never seen one before this," noted Brazen.

"It doesn't matter anyway," I said with finality. "The fact is that a raven has dark eyes and so do these things."

Brazen nodded. "Actually, that makes sense to me."

"Me, too," agreed Kix.

Great, so the two guys who had been annoying me since the day I set foot in the Netherworld PPD were now the only ones on my side. My "partner"—and yes, I use that term loosely because the jury was still out on whether or not he'd keep that title—was either being dull or obstinate. I had a feeling it was a little of both.

"Anyway," I continued my explanation of what these things were, "when Gallien Cross or one of his vampires feeds on a normal, they mix magic with the bite. This transforms the normal into kind of a vampire zombie."

"Why not just call them that?" asked Reaper. "Makes more sense."

"No," I sneered before turning back to Brazen and Kix. "Now, when they're transformed they end up with fangs, eyes that are completely black, and razor-sharp nails. They attack super fast and those nails can seriously ruin your day, but they're really weak."

While I was speaking, Dr. Hale brought up a visual on her data pad. It showed all three of the specimens that had come in from behind the warehouse and also the original woman that Reaper had sent down before.

"Creepy," Kix said with a grimace.

Brazen didn't seem to be as affected by what he saw. This didn't really surprise me seeing that he was more rough than his partner. If nothing else, that *was* one thing Brazen and I had in common.

"The point is that they're pretty easy to take out, but if you underestimate them you'll be missing your throat before you ever get the chance."

Everyone in the room nodded at that.

At least we could all agree on one thing.

"What I want to know, Doc, is if there's anything we can do to change them back before killing them?"

"I'm working on that, Piper," she replied. "One of the

doctors back in the day created an antidote, which is what I gave to this guy. It's working relatively quickly from what I can tell, but I don't know if it was ever fully tested. There's not much in the files on it, unfortunately." She shrugged. "My guess is that if I'd used it on the original woman you'd sent down it would have changed her back very quickly. This guy was fully turned. She wasn't."

"Well," I sighed, "if you get it sorted out, and we can get it into bullet mode, let me know. It'd be nice to not have to kill hundreds of these things."

"Agreed," said Reaper.

Kix's phone buzzed a moment later and he snagged it and started tapping away.

"It looks like Jax is on the move," he announced, showing his phone around. "I set it up to send me info on whenever he moves in the hopes that we'd be able to pinpoint Gallien somehow."

Impressive. I may have even raised an eyebrow and given him an appraising look. I wasn't one hundred percent sure of that because my brain was still wrestling with the possibility that these two may not be the complete boobs I'd assumed they were.

"Nice," was all I could manage. "Let's get after him."

We started out of the room after giving Hale our thanks.

I set about checking my Death Nail supply as we rode the elevator up to the main level.

"What do you want us to do while you're gone?" asked Brazen.

Just as I was about to give them another round of tasks to do here, something told me it was time to get them neck-deep in trouble. Eventually they'd have to deal with it anyway, so it may as well be now. Besides, damn it, they were doing a decent job of things.

Too bad they were dressed more like cops than Retrievers. They'd stick out like a sore thumb topside. Of course, that *could* prove to be a good thing.

"Grab your weapons," I told them. "You're coming with us."

CHAPTER 17

*J*ax walked into a null-zone shop about a mile off Canal Street. I'd had Brazen and Kix hang back from us to casually scan the area. Their goal was to have eyes on those who may have eyes on us.

The store was your standard pawn shop, except that it carried items for supers. Most of the items looked like your standard items that any pawn shop would trade in, but there were also a few items that sat outside the norm. Plasma products, for example. All legal, I assumed, since these places were constantly checked on by the local PPD.

We walked inside and started browsing.

"Do you see Jax?" I asked through the connector.

"No."

"Can you track him?"

"There's something..." He shook his head a few times. *"I can't get a lock on him. It's very dim."*

That got me to do a more active search. The place wasn't huge, but it was big enough that Jax could have been stuck between a couple of aisles. This was especially true because of his demure size.

Nothing.

Obviously something was odd about that, but there was more to this place that seemed *off*.

"*This place feels strange to me, Reap.*"

"*I feel it, too.*"

"*I usually get the tingles in null zones, but this is different. There's more to this place than meets the eye.*"

His high beams were on again. "*Agreed.*"

"Eyes," I said as I brushed past him and headed for the front counter.

The guy standing there was a djinn, which kind of seemed fitting for this area. He was covered from head to toe in tats. My favorites were the horns he had going up over each of his ears. They were shaded perfectly.

"I like the horns," I commented.

"Thanks," came the gruff reply. "What do you want?"

You would think a guy like this would relish being complimented. I'm sure he caught a lot of shit from people when he walked around. Granted, most djinn kept their ink hidden from normals, but some didn't bother. There was no rule against showing your tattoos either. The feeling was that a lot of normals got a bunch of ink done so djinn would easily blend in, as long as they didn't start causing dreams and nightmares, anyway.

"First off," I said, pointing at Reaper, "do you guys have sunglasses here?"

"Whoa," the djinn said with an impressed nod. "Those are some cool mods, pal. How'd you get that done?"

Reaper frowned.

"He's talking about your glowing eyes, Reap."

"Oh, I see," Reaper said and then turned back to the man. "My eyes were part of my build. I'm a reaper."

"Right on, man," the djinn said, clearly not catching on to what Reaper had just said. "Anyway," he added, his disposition somewhat improved, "what do you guys need?"

"A guy came in here a few minutes ago," I replied. "Small guy with black hair. Looks a bit mousey."

The djinn's face hardened and his eyes went cold.

"You cops or something?"

"Retrievers," I answered, hoping to strike some fear into the dude. "We find it interesting that he came into this building and disappeared." I leaned in. "We can't even track him, can we, Reap?"

"We cannot."

I kept my eyes on the djinn.

"See, that's a problem. If we can't track him and he's in your place of business..." I trailed off and leaned back, away from him. "Well, let's just say that it could be bad for business."

He seemed baffled. "What do you mean?"

"I mean that I'll have to unload a bunch of PPD officers on your place of business, and that probably won't look good to people who come here frequently, you know?"

His eyes were darting back and forth between me and Reaper at this point. I wouldn't say he looked so much scared as he did concerned.

"I didn't see any guy come in here," he stated finally. "You must be mistaken."

"We could always check the video feed, Piper," Reaper suggested.

He was catching on.

"Good idea. Let's do that."

"Wait," the djinn burst out. Then he licked his lips and appeared to be trying to calm himself down. "I think I remember seeing that guy. He went into the can."

"The can?" I said. "Where is it?"

The guy pointed to the back.

I nodded at him and opened a channel to Brazen and Kix.

"Guys, come on in to the pawn shop here," I commanded. *"I need you to keep an eye on this guy while we do a little hunting for Jax."*

About a minute later my two trainees walked inside and met us at the main counter.

"Keep an eye on him," I said. Then I paused and tapped on Brazen's holster. "You might want to keep that ready."

He unfastened the clip without taking his gaze off the djinn. Okay, so Brazen *could* be useful in the right circumstances. There was a rawness about him that would set most on edge.

"Kix," I said, pointing at the main door, "what say you put up the CLOSED sign until we're done in here?"

"Hey," complained the djinn. "I got a business to run here."

I spun back at him. "And if you'd like to keep it running, I suggest you let us do our thing."

To his credit, he didn't respond. He just crossed his arms and tightened his lips.

"I don't trust this guy, Brazen," I said through the

connector as Reaper and I headed back toward the bathroom. *"Keep an eye on his hands and feet. He might try to trigger something."*

"I've got it. Just find Jax."

I couldn't help but crack a smile at that. Brazen was trying to play like this was old-hat to him. Yeah, he'd been on the beat for a long time, but not as a Retriever. Maybe he'd read some of those fiction novels about us or watched one of those late-night shows. If only my life were half as glamorous as Retrievers were portrayed.

"Going in," I said as we hit the bathroom door.

It was already cracked open.

CHAPTER 18

The bathroom light was out and the room was empty. He must have slipped back out when we weren't looking, but wouldn't Reaper have picked that up?

"Reap," I said while studying the room, "could he have escaped when—"

"I would have..." He paused and shut his eyes. "I'm picking him up. It's slight, but..." He pointed at a barren wall. "That's a portal."

I stepped over to the wall and put my hand through it. Hidden zone.

"Get your gun ready," I said and then walked through.

An instant later I was standing in a tunnel. Like a tube to a cave. I had no idea where it was located, but I assumed the Netherworld Badlands. It just looked similar to that. Plus, it made sense because we would have a hard time tracking people in the Badlands.

Reaper appeared beside me.

"Badlands," he said as he reached out to touch the wall.

99

"That's my guess, but it could also just be a cave in the middle of Iowa for all we know."

"No," Reaper stated firmly. "This is definitely the Badlands." His head turned. "I sense Jax straight ahead, and he's not alone."

"How many are with him?"

"Just one." He looked up. "It's Haley."

We started creeping through the tunnel until we could hear voices. Jax and Haley were having a conversation, but I couldn't make out what they were saying.

I slowed down and walked very carefully.

Finally, their voices began to clear.

"When, Jax?" Haley said as I peered around the corner. She was pacing in front of him. "When?"

"I'll meet you tonight," he answered.

"What about the Retrievers?"

"Don't worry about them. I haven't said a thing."

His voice sounded confident. He was clearly doing his best to keep his wife alive. I couldn't blame him, and I certainly didn't want to be at fault for her death, if it was avoidable. The truth was, though, that Gallien was likely to kill both Jax and his wife anyway.

"You're certain?" Haley said.

"I will meet you at our predefined coordinates, as we agreed."

"Fine," said Haley and then she stepped back and disappeared.

Jax stood there for a moment, looking at the place Haley had just been. He was obviously tense about the entire situation. So was I, to be honest.

"*Go back,*" I whispered to Reaper.

I didn't want to connect with Jax here because there was no telling if Haley or any of the others in Gallien's crew might show up again. I just couldn't risk it.

We headed back swiftly and got to the portal, showing up on the other side and back in the bathroom.

"Now what?" asked Reaper.

"Now we step outside and act like we saw nothing in here," I said. "We don't want the shop owner to know because then he'll report back and the window will close on capturing this fucker. Plus, Jax's wife will pay the price for our knowledge."

Reaper nodded and we walked out and back to the front.

"Get him?" asked Brazen.

"No," I brooded. "He wasn't in there when we checked. We thought maybe he might have found a secret way out, but we couldn't spot anything."

The guy running the shop was noticeably pleased at hearing this. If nothing else, we had him fooled.

"Hey," Kix said, pointing toward the bathroom, "that's the guy."

Doing my best acting, I turned and looked at Jax and then pulled out my gun and pointed it at him.

He froze and put his hands up.

"Where the hell were you?" I asked.

"I was in the bathroom."

"No, you weren't," I replied sharply. "We were just in there looking around. It was empty."

"Checking up on my toilet habits?" he said, looking shaky.

"Tell us what's going on, Jax," I demanded, keeping the ruse going.

Taking my cue, Reaper added, "We can't help you if you don't help us."

Jax looked at us both with hope in his eyes. Fact was there were many more lives at stake than just his wife's.

He must have caught that in my eyes because his face turned cold.

"I already told you that I can't help you," he said. "Now, quit following me."

"But—"

"No buts," he yelled. "My wife comes first!"

"Rare for a guy to feel like that," quipped Brazen.

Everyone, including the djinn, turned and gave him a dirty look. In turn, he cleared his throat and loosened his collar.

"Sorry."

That's the Brazen I was used to.

"Asshole," I said with a smirk before refocusing on Jax. "Look, if—"

"No," Jax interrupted with a quick glance at the djinn. So he was afraid that the shop owner would squeal on him. "I'm damn sure *not* helping you."

With that proclamation, I turned to the side and motioned for him to leave.

Each of us watched him as he passed by, with the last person being Kix. Jax was out the door and signaling a taxi. He got in and headed away.

"Now what do we do?" sighed Brazen.

"I guess we're back at square one." I looked over at the

djinn. "Thanks for being less than helpful. I'm sure one day that will come back to haunt you."

"Screw you," he growled.

I sniffed and motioned my crew to leave this fine establishment.

CHAPTER 19

*W*e stepped out and I immediately sensed something was wrong.

"Do you feel that?" Reaper asked.

"Yes," I replied while scanning the area.

"Something isn't right," Brazen stated a second later while unholstering his weapon.

Another good sign. If he was feeling the same impending doom that I was, that marked him as having potential as a Retriever. That wasn't the only thing, obviously, but so far he was doing quite well. Kix was also proving himself capable on the sidekick front. His intelligence-gathering was already showing signs of promise, and I was sure if he were given the chance he'd be able to take that to the next level.

Then the world seemed to slow down as the air got more and more still.

Something was definitely off.

I heard a click.

Standing in the back of a pickup truck about a block down was Gunter, and he had a rocket launcher on his shoulder.

"Run!" I called out, but it was too late.

I saw the flash come from the muzzle of the weapon and knew there wasn't any time for us to get out of this. I couldn't even knock down any of my crew.

We were going to take the brunt of the explosion.

And we did.

The rocket slammed into a van that was parked right in front of us and all hell broke loose.

A bright blaze of light and the sound of a thousand thunder claps was the last thing I remembered until I started coming back around.

I was on my back inside the pawn shop. The windows were completely blown out and I was struggling to get my vision back on track. Everything was fading in and out, which just meant I was still healing. Given another minute or so, I'd be fine, but I had to check on everyone else and also make sure that Gunter wasn't coming to finish the job.

With a groan, I pushed myself up to an elbow and pulled out my gun.

If Gunter *did* show up, he was going to eat a few Death Nails before he took me out.

Reaper's eyes snapped open and he began to blink. He was situated between Brazen and Kix. None of them looked cut up at all, but they were still out.

"You okay?" I mumbled, my head pounding with each word.

"I'll continue to exist," he replied.

I squeezed one eye shut and nodded at the rest of my crew.

My crew?

What had the chief done to me?

"What about them?"

"They're concussed, but they should be fine," he answered as he slowly sat up. Clearly Reaper's recovery time was better than mine. "I got a shield up around us an instant before the rocket hit. If I hadn't, they'd be dead."

I forced my pained eyes open and stared at him coldly.

"What the fuck, Reap?" I implored. "Why do you keep leaving me out of the entire shield equation? I know I'm immortal, but would it kill you to think about how much of a pain it is to go through these types of events?"

"No," he replied evenly, "it would not kill me to think about that, but it would have killed them." He glanced back at Brazen and Kix as they began to stir. "Unless they're immortal, too?"

They weren't, which was *not* in their favor when it came to working as Retrievers.

To be fair, the majority of Retrievers were mortal. Or, more accurately, killable.

Just because I was immortal didn't mean I couldn't be removed from the equation without too much fuss. Stick me in an iron box, drop me in the middle of the ocean, and I was effectively dead. I was no Houdini, after all. Also, I supposed if you completely separated my head from my person that'd do it, too. I never really put much thought into it because it wasn't exactly pleasant to ponder.

"Well," I said as I stood up and started walking through

the opening that once contained a large piece of glass, "I'm going to have a chat with Gunter."

Ten steps later I heard a *click*.

Another rocket was flying, this time directly at me.

"Shields up!" I yelled. "Red alert!"

I dived to the ground and covered my head right before the rocket exploded, rocking the pawn shop. The shockwave launched me a good twenty feet farther away and I was scraped up pretty bad, but at least I was conscious this time. The dizziness I was feeling made me wish I wasn't awake, but I only had one shot at this before he loaded up another missile.

With a fair bit of effort, I scrambled forward and grabbed my gun off the sidewalk and took aim. This wasn't easy because in my stupor there appeared to be five different Gunters.

I picked the one in the middle and fired.

There was a scream, letting me know that the Death Nail had hit him. I glanced up to see that he was writhing around on the ground, having fallen out of the truck.

Good.

He wasn't dead.

Obviously, I'd hit a limb. If the Nail had struck his torso or head, he'd have died for sure.

"*Reap,*" I said through the connector, "*are you there?*"

There was no response.

Glancing back at the building showed that it had been pretty heavily damaged. There was a massive hole in its far side.

Maybe I *was* going to see what would happen to an immortal if their head was separated from their body.

That was a grim thought. All I could hope for was that he had gotten his shield up again, or that it never went down in the first place. If not, Brazen and Kix were certainly dead.

For now, I had to secure Gunter. He couldn't be allowed to get away again.

I began a drunken walk toward him.

"Move and I'll stick another Nail in you, Gunter," I said as I approached, pointing my gun at his chest. "Actually, maybe I'll do it anyway, you piece of shit."

"Fuck you," he said as he slipped something into his mouth and bit down.

His eyes went dead an instant later.

"Damn it."

I holstered my gun and knelt down beside the dead vampire. Within a minute he was headed back to Dr. Hale's.

"Doc," I said through the connector, *"I'm sending you one of the bad guys. He's dead."*

"Won't do me much good if he's dead, Piper."

"It will if you get Pecker up there to help you," I countered. "I need him to figure out how the hell they've bypassed our tracking capabilities. His arm is still intact."

"Got it."

"Also, I have a feeling you'll be getting more incoming in a few minutes, so be ready."

I leaned back against the truck that Gunter had been standing in, trying to catch my breath. Glancing over the edge, I saw his rocket launcher. With a few taps on my tattoo, it was sent off to Netherworld storage.

Then I stared over at what was left of the pawn shop, and started moving.

It was time to see if my crew was still alive.

CHAPTER 20

The place was in complete shambles as I approached, and there were normals starting to mill about.

It wasn't often that I had to put a containment call in, but it was clear I'd need to do so this time. We were asked to contact them in only the most dire circumstances, meaning lots of normals were getting a glimpse into our world. This situation seemed to fit the requirement.

"Roger," I said through the connector to our base AI, *"get a fix on my location and send a crew. We've got curious normals and a lot of damage."*

"Affirmative," came Roger's digital reply.

Reaper was already moving around, looking pretty clean, but Kix and Brazen were bloodied up this time. I rushed over and checked their pulses. Both were faint, but there.

"Reap," I called, "get your ass over here and put these two in stasis, fast."

He moaned but started dragging himself over. I grabbed his arm and helped him the rest of the way.

If I could avoid having any of my crew die on this day, that would be a good thing.

"Kix is worse off," he said tiredly as he put his hand on the man's chest and got to work.

There was nothing I could do here. I was more the type who took lives, not salvaged them.

Just in case, I headed up to the front and checked on the djinn. It was quite a mess. Imagine tattooed body parts all over the place, looking like pieces from a humanoid jigsaw puzzle.

A couple of shady-looking normals stepped through the window and started looking around. I raised my gun and walked right at them.

"Something I can help you boys with?" I barked.

They didn't need to be asked twice. The speed of their exit was legendary.

"Officer Shaw?" said a voice from behind me.

I spun and dropped to a knee, raising my gun up to find a member of the cleanup crew standing there. I lowered the weapon.

"Sorry for the mess," I said as I motioned for him and his gang to get to work. "Plenty of normals outside."

"We'll take care of it," he replied kindly.

It was nice to find people who actually enjoyed their jobs. I personally would have found it irritating as hell to have to follow up behind people like me and clean up their messes. Then again, it was probably a lot safer than being the one who made the mess.

When I got back to Reaper, Kix was already gone and Brazen was just disappearing.

Reaper stared up at me as he sat back against a wall, looking completely wiped out.

"Dr. Hale has her crew working on them both," he said. "They should be fine."

"Good," I said. "How are you?"

"Exhausted, but I'll recover."

His eyes were very dim. If only he could keep them like that all the time, they wouldn't be so bad. I decided not to make that suggestion.

"Gunter?" he asked.

"Shot him in the arm."

"I'm impressed," Reaper said with a tilt of his head. "I thought you would have killed him outright. It will be good to get information from him."

"Yeah, about that..." I replied while watching the cleanup crew deal with the normals, "he bit down on something and killed himself."

"Ah."

"Whatever it is Gallien and his crew are trying to accomplish, it seems to be worth dying over."

Reaper swallowed and then coughed pretty hard. I went to help him, but he held out a hand to stop me. It took him a few moments to catch his breath.

"I'm okay," he said, "but thanks. Just have some shards of glass in my lungs."

Anyone else would *not* be okay in that scenario.

"We should get you to Dr. Hale, too," I said. "I know you'll heal on your own, but a little help couldn't hurt.

Besides, we need to check on the others and see if Pecker is going to be able to crack Gunter's tattoo."

"Huh?"

"We can't track them, remember?" I then remembered who I was talking to. "Okay, *average* Retrievers can't track them, and even you can't do it unless they're nearby. I sent Gunter's body down so Pecker could get a look at his tattoo."

"I see."

"*Dr. Hale,*" I called back to base, "*Reap is going to come down for a quick check.*"

"*We've already got our hands full, Piper.*"

"*So just give him a pain shot or something,*" I commanded. "*He'll heal on his own, but he needs a little help.*"

There was no response, but she'd do it.

"Go Reap," I said. "I'll be down in a second. I just want to have a deeper look around first."

He disappeared.

There wasn't likely to be anything in the pawn shop that could be of much use, but I walked back to the main counter and began studying the area. My hope was that I'd at least find out if the djinn had some way of communicating with Gallien. If he did, maybe Pecker could find a way to pinpoint the prick.

The djinn's lower half was mostly intact, so I went through his jeans, which was pretty damn nasty. I nearly barfed, in fact. All I found for my trouble was a wallet with an ID card, two dollar bills, and a condom that looked like it had probably expired ten years ago.

The counter was so blown to bits that even if there

had been a button or some other way of communication, it was long gone by now.

I supposed that it could be possible for them to have a form of connector like we had. If Pecker could do that for Reaper, then whoever hacked these tattoos could likely to do the same for Gallien and his goons.

Fun.

Just as I was about to head back down to the Netherworld, I caught sight of a case that had somehow survived the explosion. This was probably because it was seated back behind a large concrete wall on the side opposite where the rocket had struck.

I walked over and reached inside, smiling.

CHAPTER 21

*I*t was against protocol to transport directly to any place in the Netherworld PPD unless you had an immediate need, so I had to hit the main portal.

Just as I stepped off and headed for the elevator, Chief Carter cut me off.

"What in the blazes is going on, Piper?" he said with a bit of heat. "Dr. Hale's doing what she can to save Kix and Brazen, who were under *your* protection, a building in the Overworld has been compromised, and I've got the head of the containment department griping at me regarding the extent of the damage up there!"

I nodded at him. "Sounds like you've got the latest details all sewn up fine, Chief."

"Don't get smart with me, young lady," he replied, wagging his finger. "I want answers and I want them now."

"I'm not sure what you want me to say. We're trying to catch this guy and he's got a lot of goons who are carrying a fair amount of firepower. Oh, and we can't track them.

At least not at a distance." I was doing my best to keep my voice under control. "As for Brazen and Kix, I warned you that—"

He waved his hand at me. "I don't need your explanations about them. They'll be fine, and even if they aren't, they knew what they were getting into."

"Then why are you so fired up?"

"Because the head of the containment department is a real nag, that's why." He grunted. "I *hate* dealing with her."

"But you're married to her, Chief," I noted with a frown.

"Exactly my point."

I wanted to laugh, but I was already in enough trouble.

"Look, Chief," I said finally, "I'm doing everything I can to contain Gallien, but he's not making it easy."

"That may be, but—"

"You put me on the toughest cases for a reason, Chief," I reminded him.

He glared at me for a second and then sighed. Then he turned and skulked back to his office.

"Catch him, Piper," he yelled over his shoulder. "Soon!"

The volume of his last word was enough to make me shake slightly. I loved the guy, and he *did* look rather jolly —even when he was mad, but something always told me that he was not to be trifled with too much. There was just a depth in the way he carried himself that told me there lived a badass under all that grandfatherliness.

I jumped on the elevator and hit the medical level.

When I walked into the room, I saw that Brazen was still being worked on. Kix was in a seated position, breathing on his own.

Keeping to the periphery, I scooted over to where Reaper was seated.

"How are you feeling?" I asked.

"Nearly healed," he slurred. "Thanks for getting the doc to medsi...meder...uh..."

"Medicate?" I suggested.

"Yeah, that," he said, grinning serenely. "It feels wonderful."

Great, Dr. Hale had managed to turn a once-reaper into an instant junkie.

"What the hell did you give Reap, Doc?" I asked as she sped past.

"Ibuprofen," she replied.

"That's it?" I rasped, wide-eyed.

There was no answer as I turned back to stare at Reaper, who appeared to be on cloud nine.

"Lightweight," I chuckled, and then said, "Are you with it at all, Reap, or should we talk later?"

"Am I with what?" he asked, turning to face me. He cracked a warm smile. "You're a good friend, Piper."

"Oh boy."

"No, I mean it," he said. "I don't have many friends." Then he pursed his lips. "I mean, Brazen is okay."

"He is?" I asked, shocked that Reaper, or *anyone*, would think that. "I doubt his own mother thinks he's okay, Reap."

"And I like Kix, too," he continued, clearly ignoring my comment. "Rough arbout...abround...*around* the edges, I guess. But he's okay."

"Uh-huh."

"The chief is great, too."

I couldn't argue that. My life would have been vastly different were it not for the chief.

"And Dr. Hale and I went to dinner once." It was hard to tell, but it *looked* like his eyes were pulsing. "She was nice. It wasn't meant to be, though." He patted my arm. "Love is a pickle thing, you know."

"I think you mean 'fickle,' Reap."

He furrowed his brow for a moment and then shrugged.

"Got it," exclaimed Pecker from across the room, causing me to jump.

Reaper giggled. "I love Pecker," he confided. "Honestly, Pecker is great."

I wanted to tease him again about his choice of words, but I found it more amusing this way. If I went about correcting him each time, he'd figure it out and stop saying things without first thinking them through. Where was the fun in that?

"Here," I said as I got up to go and talk with Pecker, "I got you something."

I showed him the pair of sunglasses I'd taken from the case at the pawn shop, and dropped them in his lap.

"Aw," he said as he slowly put them on. "I love them, Piper."

The glow of his eyes disappeared.

Good enough for me.

"What's up?" I said to Pecker as I approached.

"This guy's tat is quite a piece of work," he said. "There's definitely a tracking mechanism in it."

Shit.

"Do you think Gallien was informed that he was down here?"

"No," he said. "The tat is powered by the owner's energy or external energy, so it went inert when he died, but I was able to run a passive check to find the tracking system before I ran power through to it."

"Good," I breathed.

"Anyway, it's got some pretty crazy stuff going on in here. Decent tracking, communications, their own portal setup." He rubbed his chin. "Honestly, it's better than my creations on many fronts."

That was quite an admission from the chief engineer in the Netherworld PPD.

"Can we use it to find Gallien?"

"Hmmm?" he said and then looked up at me. "Oh, yeah, yeah. Definitely. I'll have something running on this soon and will get you their coordinates."

"Being able to track them would be quite helpful," I said.

"Can't do any realtime tracking in a short amount of time, Piper," he said, "but I should be able to get his current location based on the history data in this guy's tat."

"Oh, I see," I said. "What about communications and using their portals?"

"Not likely," he admitted. "There's a lot of code in here and it's all pretty heavily encrypted. Again, though, I should be able to get you the whereabouts on at least one of them within an hour or two."

It'd have to do.

Just before I turned to leave, I remembered that Pecker

had stuck the rune that I brought back earlier into his comparison machine.

"What about the rune?" I said. "Any matches?"

"Oh yeah. No matches on the magic front, but the computer found a ninety-seven percent hit on a wizard."

That was odd. Both Reaper and Pecker pointed out how it was nearly impossible to match someone's painting strokes, coloring, shading, etc., and I already knew that magical signatures were unique.

"How is that possible?"

"I thought it was odd, too," he answered with a shrug. "The painting was almost dead-on, but the magic was completely different."

"Strange."

"Yeah."

"So," I asked, "anyone we know?"

Pecker looked at the readout. "Azura."

"Never heard of him," I said.

"It's a her, not a him," corrected Pecker, "and according to her files, she's kind of a tool."

Considering that she was involved in helping these pricks, that was an understatement.

CHAPTER 22

A few hours later, everyone was back on their feet and cleared for action. There was nothing quite like being a supernatural and having a set of doctors like Hale and her staff.

"How are you two feeling?" I asked Brazen and Kix.

I already knew Reaper was fine, and thankfully his ibuprofen had faded enough to make him sober again. I would have to keep him away from the drugstore for sure. Having an ibuprofen-head on my hands would not only be annoying, it'd be embarrassing.

"Feeling a little foggy," admitted Kix, "but I should be okay."

Brazen stood tall and said, "Never better," but I could see he was still in a heap of discomfort.

"When will you be ready for action?"

"Now," Brazen answered immediately.

Kix looked at him like he was nuts, and then his eyes darted about for a second.

"Yeah," he said as if he were catching on to how things worked in Retriever land. "I'm ready to go when you are."

"Good," I stated, though Reaper didn't seem too happy with my quick movement on this issue. "We got word back from Pecker that he's found the location of Gallien's stronghold."

I clicked on my screen and zoomed the map out until we were looking down near the docks in New Orleans. It was a nondescript building that appeared to be abandoned. At least, there weren't any cars around to signal otherwise. In fact, the entire area was kind of barren.

"Did he give any details on what kind of army we're looking at in there?" asked Brazen.

"No, but I'm assuming it's not going to be a walk in the park." I leaned back and crossed my arms. "That said, my guess is that if we cut out their leader, the rest of them will either take off or surrender."

Kix nodded. "Still, shouldn't we have backup?"

My eye twitched.

"Piper doesn't believe in backup," Reaper chimed in. "They 'get in the way.'"

"No need for finger-quotes, Reap. Backup *does* get in the way." I motioned at the three of them. "For example, I could have been at Gallien's building thirty minutes ago if I hadn't been stuck here waiting for you guys."

"You really *do* prefer to go at it alone, don't you?" Reaper asked in a non-sarcastic way.

"Less responsibility," I answered.

He grunted and shook his head at me.

"All right," I went on before there could be any debate

on the subject, "I'm going to give you two the option to take a pass on this." I was kind of hopeful here. I'd had to wait for them in order to ask, but they could turn down the offer without punishment from me. "There's no negative points for staying here. I've already seen you through some pretty bad shit, so it won't influence my decision about your entry into the RTP if you want—"

"We're going," Brazen interrupted.

"Yeah, Piper," Kix said just as firmly. "We started this and we need to finish it."

"You both realize that you could die, right?" I pointed back and forth between me and Reaper. "We're both immortal. You two...not so much."

"We know what we are," said a determined Brazen. "So are we going or not?"

"Fine," I said, staring back and forth at them, "but you have to put on some decent garb and get some proper weaponry. Your basic cop shit just doesn't cut it."

CHAPTER 23

With Brazen and Kix properly dressed and armed, we were ready to take a trip to the building that Gallien and his crew were supposedly holed up in.

"I like the brown tweed, Brazen," I said. "It kind of has that used-car salesman thing going. Suits you."

"Yeah?" he smirked. "Thanks, Piper."

All right. I guess he'd been going for that look, then. Honestly, it *did* fit his personality.

Kix, on the other hand, went with the charcoal gray and a hat that was similar to Reaper's. Then I caught something interesting about his hat. He had a black feather sticking off the side of it.

I was going to comment but decided to let it go.

"Okay," I said, taking my gun out, "get your weapons ready and don't do anything stupid." Just as I was about to head in, I stopped and added, "In other words, do *not* fire your weapons unless there is no other option."

"You want to take them alive?" asked Kix.

"Uh…sure," I answered. Then I decided it was time for a teaching moment, so I paused. "Think of it like a stakeout. You don't want the bad guys to know you're keeping tabs on them, right?"

Brazen just stared at me.

"Right," I said. "Well, once you guys have a warrant, you break in with guns high and voices yelling."

"Exactly," said Kix. "Guessing you don't want that here, though, because these guys aren't likely to roll over easily."

I nodded at him and said, "And so we are going to sneak in as best as we can. At some point it'll be obvious that we arrived, but let's try to at least get an idea for the layout of the place before that happens."

Brazen motioned at his jacket. "You think dressing like this will help us blend in?"

Reaper chuckled at that. His sunglasses probably wouldn't help either. They were better than his glowing eyes, though.

"Just follow me," I said and then started hugging the walls. *Reap, I'm guessing you're tracking?*

"Yes," he replied through the connector.

He was learning.

We moved along carefully. I doubted there were any cameras in place to detect intruders, but it was possible. If there were, I couldn't see any. A more likely scenario would be sentries or runes. Runes were most probable since we'd already seen a few of them during our fun hunting Gallien.

Since I was the only one in our little troop who could spot runes, I kept my eyes opened and scanning.

"Body just around this corner," Reaper said. *"Female, about your build. She's carrying a gun."*

I held up a hand to stop them as I took the next few steps and peered around the corner. In a flash, I jumped out and threw a left cross right to her temple. She dropped instantly.

"Kix," I called while crouching down and checking the woman's pockets, *"send this one down to holding, and give them instructions to block her tattoo. My gut tells me she doesn't have the same tweaks as the others we've seen, but better not to chance it."*

"You got it, boss," he said.

I couldn't help but notice Brazen's sour look at Kix calling me "boss." That worked for me—both being called "boss" by Kix, and Brazen not liking it, I mean. Good stuff.

"Oh," I caught myself, *"also tell them to read her the Retriever bit."*

He looked up. *"The what?"*

"They'll know, and with any luck, you'll learn it soon enough."

The guard shimmered from view and we moved on.

"Two more, straight ahead," announced Reaper.

I motioned Kix and Brazen to go wide and then stepped up with Reaper in tow. The goal was simple. Reaper and I get spotted, the bad guys turn toward us, Kix and Brazen knock them on the head and down they go. This was a standard cop play, so my hope was there wouldn't be any hiccups. If anything went wrong, I had Death Nails to make it right.

"Hey," the one guard said, turning toward us.

This caught the attention of the other guard. By the time he had his gun up, though, he was out. If there was any one thing I had to hand to Brazen, it was his ability to knock the crap out of somebody. The guard by Kix had been dropped, too, though it wasn't as fluid.

"*Send them down,*" I said. "*Reap, anyone else on track?*"

He held up his finger as his head moved around as if using sonar. Chances were that's exactly what he was doing, except through energy signatures. Each person had a unique signature, so if Reap had catalogued one in the past, he could track it whenever it was nearby. Send out a wave and see what energy bounces back. If it matched a signature he had in his mental filing cabinet, he'd know who it was.

Again, that was a guess.

"*Gallien, Haley, Jax, and a woman I don't recognize are in a room up ahead,*" he said, pointing. "*There are a few more guards along the way, though.*"

"*Got it.*" My guess was that the woman was Jax's wife. Getting her and Jax out was admittedly unlikely, but it was worth a shot. "*Let's clear those guards and get in there before Gallien does anything stupid.*"

"*You mean like make a bunch of vampire zombies?*" asked Reaper.

I gave him the evil eye. "*I thought we agreed to call them ravens?*"

"I *never agreed to that,*" he argued. "*I still think that's a silly name for them.*"

"*No sillier than the name Reaper for a reaper,*" I mumbled. "*Asshat.*"

I waved everyone forward and we got moving.

CHAPTER 24

*W*e dropped a few more guards as we approached the room that Gallien was in. I nodded at the other three and got ready to push through the doors, when Reaper stopped me.

"Would you mind using these instead of Death Nails?" he asked while holding up Numbshots. *"There's no need to kill everyone in there, especially not Gallien."*

Numbshots were standard bullets used by most Retrievers. Their purpose was to numb instead of kill. If you got hit by one of them in the leg, for example, you'd be dragging your leg around like a dead weight within seconds. Kind of like when you have a limb that falls asleep. It's not dead, but you just can't properly control it. If you hit someone in the torso with a Numbshot, it would put everything to sleep except for their head. If you hit them in the head, they'd likely die. It *was* still a bullet, after all.

I blinked at him. *"Why?"*

"Because a one-hundred-percent commission is much better

than a twenty-five-percent commission, Piper," he replied evenly.

"Thanks for the math lesson," I said. *"But so what?"*

"So what? So I have bills to pay, that's what." He was looking at me like I was an idiot. *"My rent is due, I've got groceries to buy, my pet turtle has a vet appointment that I have to pay for, my—"*

"Wait," I said, lowering my gun, *"you have a pet turtle?"*

He tilted his head to the side. *"Yes, why?"*

"Exactly my question," I replied. *"Why do you have a pet turtle?"*

"Because when I was learning to live in your world, it was suggested I find a pet that was relatively easy to take care of," he answered. *"They said it would help me to understand the emotional ties that your kind have to creatures here."*

"But why a turtle?" said Brazen. *"Why not get a dog or something?"*

"Again, Officer Brazen," Reaper said, *"it needed to be a pet that was easy to maintain."*

"Cats are pretty easy to manage," Kix noted. We all looked at him. *"What? I've got two cats. They're not a problem."*

I didn't know why, but somehow seeing Kix as a cat-person kind of made sense. He even had a few tattoos of kittens on his neck, which made him look like a somewhat sensitive djinn. Brazen, on the other hand, was a dog-person all the way. It was obvious by looking at him that he probably had a couple of Rottweilers or even Great Danes hanging around his house.

In the grand scheme of things, I didn't give a damn what kind of animals they had, but a vision of Reaper sitting on his couch watching Oprah while holding his pet turtle flashed through my mind.

I snorted and then caught myself.

"What's his name?" I asked.

"Her *name is Agnes,"* he answered without inflection.

"Agnes?"

"That's right."

I had to literally bite my lip to keep from smiling.

"Okay," I said after getting myself under control. *"Well, I'll tell you what,"* I added as I looked back at the bullets he was holding, *"if you want to use those Numbshots and you can knock out Gallien with them, be my guest. I'm going to stick with the Death Nails."*

"You know I don't like using guns, Piper," he stressed.

"I do know that, Reap, yes. But as long as you don't hit anyone in the head with a Numbshot, you won't kill them." Then I gave him a look. *"And remember how you essentially obliterated everyone with your energy blast in the courtyard?"* He winced. *"Yeah,"* I admonished, *"I wouldn't go out of my way to get on a high horse about how guns are too deadly."*

"That wasn't my fault."

"I can accept that," I concurred, *"but now that you know what that energy pulse can do, are you going to use it again?"*

He hesitated.

I smiled.

"That's what I thought."

Then I held up my gun and cracked open the door for a look inside.

Reaper grabbed my arm.

"Wait," he warned. *"There are nearly one hundred forms in there."* He grabbed his head and began moving back and

forth as if he were in pain. *"Many of them are vampire zom...
ravens."* His breathing was ragged. *"They are all very angry.
Controlled, but angry."*

"Reap," I said, grabbing one of his arms and pulling it
away from his head, *"stop."*

He jolted.

"What the hell just happened?" I asked.

It took him a second to catch his breath.

*"Sometimes when I track, the emotions of my prey sink in
and I can get consumed by it."* He swallowed. *"As a reaper, it's
something I could easily disassociate from. But in this form,
separating myself from the emotion is not as easy."*

At some point, he and I were going to have to have a
long talk about all of his idiosyncrasies. Assuming we
were going to remain partners, that was. My vote on this
subject was still out with my internal jury, but I had a
feeling Chief Carter was going to try and make this a
permanent situation. If that happened, I'd need to know
what kind of weird shit was going on in Reaper's head
before we were put into situations...well, like this one.

"Are you going to be able to handle this, Reap?" I asked
directly. *"If not, you're going back to base."*

"I'll be fine," he said in a tired voice. *"I just can't track
those things in large groups like that."*

"Okay." I gave him another glance and grunted. *"We
already know what's behind this door, so you don't need to track
anything until we take them all out."*

"You're going to kill all of—"

"Not if I can help it," I interrupted.

That was another thing we were going to have a talk
about. These were life-and-death situations...or at least

very-painful-wait-to-heal   types-but-don't-really-die-because-you're-immortal situations. Anyway, the point was that I wasn't fond of having to deal with Reaper acting as my conscience when I was facing shit like this.

"Look," I lectured, "*if we can take out Gallien, Haley, and I'm assuming Phillip, then the ravens should all just fall down because they won't be controlled anymore.*"

"*You sure about that?*" asked Brazen.

"*Not even slightly,*" I admitted. "*In fact, I'll be damn surprised if it happens that way, but it's worth a shot.*"

Nobody said anything.

It was time for a fight.

CHAPTER 25

There were definitely a lot of bodies in the room when we walked in, guns held high.

It was one thing to have a hundred cops facing a hundred naughties, but it was quite another to have four cops doing it.

All faces turned to look at us.

"Ah, Officer Shaw," Gallien said with a genuine smile. "I have to say that I'm surprised to see you here. You definitely have balls."

"That makes one of us," I replied and then frowned as I realized that comment didn't really reflect positively on me. "Damn it."

"I'm assuming you have surrounded the building with officers?" he asked.

I glanced at Reaper. Okay, so maybe this *was* an instance where having backup wouldn't have been a bad idea. Yes, I expected that Gallien would have ravens with him but I didn't think there'd be this many.

Gallien began to laugh. "You *don't* have backup?" He

slapped his leg. "Well, then I must say you really *do* have balls!" After a moment he wiped his eyes. "You're also incredibly stupid, I might add."

"Hard to argue that," mumbled Brazen.

I gave him a warning stare.

"What?" he said. *"It's true."*

"Brazen," I seethed, *"why don't you spend your time aiming your fucking weapon at Gallien, Haley, or Phillip, and pulling the trigger?"*

"Oh, right."

We all pointed our guns at the brass standing up on the platform who overlooked the sea of ravens.

Jax was standing with them, too, and there was a woman with him as well. She looked to be a bit older than him and she had straggly white hair. Her face was impassive, which just spelled to me that she'd already accepted her fate.

"What say we cut the shit, Gallien?" I called out to him. "We may not be able to kill all of your ravens, but we can certainly—"

"My what?" he interrupted, frowning.

"Ravens," I responded while waving my gun at the mass of black-eyed creatures between us. "That's what I call these things you've created."

"They're Vampire Zombies, Officer Shaw," he corrected. "You'd think that would be obvious."

I pointed at my crew with my free hand, but I didn't look at them.

"Not a word out of you three."

They didn't say anything, but I could sense what they were thinking.

"Anyway, Cross," I continued, "we can either do this the easy way or the hard way. Which would you prefer?"

"By all means, Officer Shaw," he answered with a grand smile, "the hard way."

My reply to his smug face was to fire a Death Nail right at his forehead.

It hit a shield and fell to the ground.

He laughed again.

"You *had* to know I was going to be protected, Officer Shaw," he said with a laugh. "Honestly, I'd expected far more from you than this."

"*Me, too,*" said Brazen.

"That was just a check, Gallien," I responded, ignoring Brazen. "Now that I know you've got another rune somewhere about, I'll just have to destroy it and then your ass is grass."

His smile faded instantly as he glanced over at the wall. There was the rune I was hoping to see.

It was my turn to grin.

Gallien's eyes burned and he yelled, "Kill them!"

CHAPTER 26

I dived to the right and rolled back up to my feet, taking off at a full run.

It was only a matter of time before the ravens got to me so I needed to knock out that rune fast.

Hissing filled the room, along with angry grunts and screeches. The damn things *sounded* like ravens. I wanted to snark something back through the connector, but the cracking of gunfire told me my crew was neck-deep in fighting off claws and teeth.

I ducked as an arm swiped at me, doing its best to dislodge my head from my person.

A quick fire of my gun ended that attack.

But I could see I was being cut off and so I slowed and turned, firing round after round into the oncoming faces. I hadn't wanted to kill any of the damn things, but it was either that or end up falling to their ripping hands. Something told me I wouldn't survive full dismemberment. Plus, if I fell, that would be one less person Gallien had to worry about, which would likely spell the end of my crew.

Not on my watch.

With practiced precision, I started firing.

Nails burst through chests and skulls like a knife through butter. Fortunately, the Nails were working as intended on these beasts, which was a worry considering they weren't fully turned. Ravens dropped left and right as I emptied my magazine repeatedly.

The nice thing about Death Nails was that each magazine carried fifty of them. The shitty thing about Death Nails magazines was that they tended to get stuck during changes, assuming you didn't take your time.

I ejected the mag while simultaneously snatching a fresh one from my jacket. This I could do with haste. The next step was a slow entry back into the base of the gun. It was either that or the damn thing would get stuck. I couldn't tell you how many times I'd argued with Pecker about this. His default reaction was always that he had more important things to work on and that I shouldn't be putting myself in these situations anyway.

By the time the mag was fully seated, I had a raven right on me.

Fortunately, I remembered they were weak.

Claws raked at my head, but I ducked and bumped the creature headfirst into the wall. The sound it made was just like the one I'd heard back when I'd killed the raven down near the docks.

Another lurched through the air with its hands waving wildly.

I ducked.

It died.

That's when I resumed firing while doing my best to get to that damned rune.

Out of the corner of my eye I saw movement on the stage. Gallien and his gang were taking off.

"*Shit*," I yelled through the connector, "*they're getting away.*"

"*Don't seem to be trying to get away,*" Brazen grunted in response. "*Fucking things are everywhere.*"

"*I'm talking about Gallien.*"

I started thinking that getting to the rune really didn't matter all that much at this point.

That's when a claw caught me on the back of my head, spinning me hard to the ground. The damn things could punch, that was for sure.

It was time to get seriously bad-ass on these fuckers.

I started firing in double time, off my back, clearing just enough room to launch myself back to my feet. Then I started going into full fight-mode. That meant hands, feet, teeth, Death Nails, and anything I had at my disposal to maim and kill.

"You dicks want to hit me?" I roared as the sting of fresh cuts burned the back of my head. "Well, then let's play."

Like a woman possessed, I got into the fray.

I brought a left roundhouse kick up, catching one of the ravens on the cheek. Blood spurted from its mouth as it tumbled to the ground.

Continuing my motion, I spun and back-fisted

another in the throat. It choked as I put my gun to its head and sent him off to the reapers.

Claws struck my arm, digging in firmly.

I swore and then yanked free, littering the attacker with Death Nails. One would have been enough, but I was pissed. He fell back, dead, as the next one dived over him.

I lunged forward, getting close to my attacker so her claws couldn't do as much damage. Once we connected, my hand was on her throat, twisting and pulling with such ferociousness that I nearly took her head off.

Instinctively, I dropped to a knee and another of the ravens flew overhead. He didn't hit a wall, but he did slam into one of his pals, which bought me a little time to spin and release a couple of Nails into the crowd.

The ravens were thinning, but there were still too many of them and I was starting to get tired.

"Anyone have any Empirics?" I exclaimed hopefully.

"I have two," Reaper replied.

So he could use Empirics, but guns were uncivilized? That was one odd dude.

"Brazen and Kix, get the hell out of here right now," I commanded while throwing another Raven at the wall. *"Reaper, launch those Empirics."*

"We're not going anywhere, Piper," Brazen shot back.

"The fuck you aren't," I snapped. *"You can't survive the Empirics. We can. Now get the hell out!"*

A raven tackled me, followed by another landing on top of him. Within seconds, I was trapped under a mass of swinging claws and gnashing teeth. It was all I could do to protect my neck and head.

"Throw them," I screamed at the top of my lungs.

The world suddenly lit up like a thousand bolts of lightning had erupted in the room.

Pain ripped through my body with such power that getting shredded by claws was almost preferable in comparison.

Then everything went black.

CHAPTER 27

$\mathcal{I}$ woke up to find Brazen pulling bodies off of me. Even though my vision was blurred and wavering, I could see the look of concern on his face.

"I got you, Piper," he said, putting my head on his lap as he pushed my hair out of my eyes. "You'll be all right. Let me just get you some meds."

He reached into his pocket and pulled out a bottle of something I'd never seen before. I held up my hand to stop him.

"I'll heal," I choked. "Thanks, though."

Brazen nodded slowly and put the bottle back.

This wasn't some odd thing where the guy thought I was smoking hot or anything, and it wasn't one of those damsel-in-distress situations either. I hated those. I was just a fellow officer and Brazen was doing his best to make sure I survived. Just like I'd done for him.

Again, he was proving himself to be solid Retriever material.

Good.

147

"Help me up," I said.

By the time I was on my feet, so was Reaper. Kix was standing with him.

"Thanks, Brazen," I whispered while the world fought to right itself. "I appreciate it."

"You're a cop. I'm a cop. It's what we do."

Valid.

The fact was that when you dedicated your life to the protection of others, you became part of a fraternity. You could razz each other, despise each other, and be downright douchy to each other when in the office, but when there were bad guys about, you were a team. Period.

That entire "protection of others" thought was suddenly haunting me as I scanned around at the mass of bodies lying on the floor.

They were all normals. Slightly turned, yes, but normals nonetheless. It sucked.

"Reaper," I said as we stepped over the corpses and headed over toward the stage that Gallien had previously occupied, "can you locate them anywhere?"

He nodded his head and pointed toward a door at the back as he and Kix moved to catch up with us.

Then he added, "I thought Pecker updated our tattoos for tracking them?"

"You're right," I said, pulling up my sleeve and getting a fix on Gallien. Then I stopped and held out my arm to stop the others. "Wait a second. There may be more ravens in there."

I started looking around for other entrances.

Nothing.

Then I looked up at the ceiling tiles.

"What are you thinking, Piper?" Reaper asked dubiously.

"I'm thinking that you guys are going to go in there with guns drawn," I replied, studying the area. "You'll talk with them, stalling as best you can, as I climb across the ceiling."

"And what if there are a bunch of ravens, like you said?" asked Kix.

Reaper held up his hand, closed his eyes, and concentrated. It didn't look like he was having much fun doing it either. If his head felt anything like mine, I could understand why.

"There are none," Reaper panted as Kix held him from falling over. "It's just Gallien, Haley, Phillip, Jax, and Jax's wife."

I nodded. "Perfect."

This was going to be a challenge for sure, and chances were that my crew was going to be walking into an unfortunate situation. Another glance around at the mass of bodies reminded me that this wasn't anything new.

"Do you have enough energy to put a shield around these two?" I asked while nodding at Brazen and Kix.

Reaper shook his head. "I don't think so. I'm barely functioning now."

"Okay, you guys are staying out here then."

"And leaving Reaper to go in on his own?" Brazen said with a not-so-funny laugh. "Uh, no."

"That's a direct order, Brazen."

"Fuck you, Piper," he said. "I'm not letting a fellow officer go in there without backing him up."

"I agree," Kix stated firmly. "It's not right."

I crossed my arms and glared at them both. It was difficult to chastise them for what they were saying, but it was also my job to keep them alive.

"You'll both stay out here and that's final."

Brazen crossed his arms back. "Nope."

"Sorry, Piper," Kix agreed. "We just can't do that."

There was no time to fight with these two over this. I had no idea what Gallien was planning in there, but my assumption was that it couldn't be good.

We had to move.

Now.

"Fine," I replied with heat, "but if you get yourselves killed, it's on you, not me."

"We'll remember that," Brazen said.

I shook my head at him.

"Asshole."

CHAPTER 28

I got up into the rafters with a bit of help and then started crawling along.

"*Remember, Reap,*" I instructed, directly at him through the connector, "*let them think I'm dead.*"

"Right."

"*If you can shield Brazen and Kix at any point, do it.*" I then added, "*If you have to choose one, I'd say—*"

"*Don't go there, Piper,*" he cut me off. "*We're walking in.*"

I stuck to the beam that was running along the ceiling so I wouldn't make any sound to the room below. The goal was to drop in on them, which wouldn't be possible if I gave myself away.

"All right, Gallien," I heard Reaper say, his voice sounding pretty weak, "by order of the Netherworld Retrievers, I, Reaper Payne, and my crew here, place you under arrest, and we shall transport you back to the Netherworld and present you before the Tribunal for sentencing."

I heard the sound of a golf clap.

"Bravo," said Gallien. "Honestly, I'm impressed at the fact that you three made it through my vampire zombies."

I grunted at that.

"I see that Officer Shaw is not with you though," he said in mock sadness. "Such a shame. She *was* a joy to run from."

"Are you going to come willingly," Reaper started, ignoring Gallien's teasing, "or do we have to kill you?"

"You'll most definitely have to kill me," Gallien replied seriously. "I do think you'll find that a bit challenging, though. Again, there is a shield up and your pathetic bullets just can't penetrate it. Honestly, you guys are just terrible at this game."

"Look for a rune board," I instructed.

"I can't see runes, remember?" Reaper responded.

Damn it.

"Okay, look for any *board that seems to be out of place."*

"Got it," he said. *"It's on the right wall as you walk in the room, about halfway between us and them."*

"Good."

I continued forward and saw a bit of light peeking up through one of the tiles. With careful movement, I lowered myself and peered through.

Directly beneath me was Jax and his wife. Standing before them were the combined front of Gallien, Haley, and Phillip. Haley was holding up an Empiric.

"She has an—"

"An Empiric," I interrupted Reaper. *"I know. I see it. Stall them for another second."*

"Right." Reaper then spoke aloud. "Okay, okay," he said. "We'll put down our weapons."

"We'll what?" said Brazen.

"Do it, Officer Brazen," Reaper commanded. "You too, Kix."

I could only see my crew's legs from my vantage point, but pretty soon there were three guns on the floor by their feet.

"There," Reaper said. "Now there's no reason to throw that Empiric. We can't harm you."

Gallien laughed. "You couldn't harm us before, you idiot."

He had a point.

"Why are you doing this?" asked Brazen. "Are you just some ball hair whose mother didn't give him enough love and whose daddy wouldn't take him to a baseball game or something?"

The air fell still.

"Excuse me?" Gallien replied with coldness in his voice.

"I'm just wondering why you turned out to be such a sweaty pube. Had to be shitty parenting or an uncle who touched you inappropriately, maybe?"

I got back to my feet and glanced down at the tiles. None of them could contain my weight, so if I jumped on one, I should fall straight through and land in the expanse between Jax and Gallien. Of course, I could also just fire Death Nails down at them, right?

If the shield only covered their front, that would work great. If not, my cover would be blown.

No, I was going to have to jump. I holstered my gun, snapped two Death Nails out of a mag, palmed them, and got ready.

"Let me tell you something, you insignificant worm," Gallien began. "I never met my parents because—"

"Ah," interrupted Brazen. "You were an orphan. Makes sense why you're such a curly hair, then."

What was with him and pubic hairs?

"Enough of this," Gallien seethed. "Haley—"

That was all he got out as I crashed through the ceiling and landed behind them.

They spun, but I drove the Nails into Gallien and Phillip with one swift move.

Both of them screamed and fell over.

So much for that full commission.

Haley launched the Empiric at my crew just as I tackled her. The squelched explosion told me that Reaper had taken yet another one for the team. Honestly, I was starting to think he enjoyed the pain.

I punched the living shit out of Haley, knocking out teeth and bloodying her up until she passed out. If she was still alive after my savage beating, I'd be surprised.

Finally, I stood up and walked over to the rune board and kicked it, breaking it in two.

"*Did you kill Gallien?*" Reaper groaned through the connector. "*Tell me you didn't kill Gallien.*"

"*Uh...*" I cleared my throat. "*Let's just say I'll lend you whatever you need to pay your rent.*"

He groaned again.

"Well, Jax," I said as I approached the little man and his wife. "Looks like this is over for you."

"I don't know how to thank you," he said with elation on his face.

"It wasn't just me," I said, turning back to my crew as

Kix and Brazen did their best to get Reaper back to his feet. "These guys did—"

A shot was fired.

It struck me right in the middle of my back, throwing me forward and leaving me flat on my face in agony.

For the second time that night, the world faded from view.

CHAPTER 29

*D*on't let anyone fool you, being immortal kind of sucks, because every time you pass out from being injured, you wake back up during the healing process and get to feel the entire thing. And it doesn't matter how grievous the injury is, either. Getting shot right in the goddamn spine, for example.

I couldn't move yet, but my ears were working fine.

"I can't believe how stupid you all are," said the voice of Jax. "Falling for the my-wife-is-in-their-clutches-and-they're-going-to-kill-her bit? Seriously. You're a bunch of idiots."

Damn it.

"So this entire thing was a setup to kill us?" asked Kix.

"Don't flatter yourself," Jax replied with a laugh. "You four aren't worth that. This was all done so I could build my army."

"What about Gallien?"

Jax grunted.

"He was my second in command, but I had to let him

run the show once I decided to play you fools. I couldn't risk you finding out beforehand."

"Let me ask you something," said Brazen with an edge, "did your parents not love you as a child or something?"

Good lord. Did he only have one trick?

"I'm not going for that game," Jax said an instant before the popping of a gun being fired sounded.

There was a thump and then the thud of a body falling.

I knew the sound of that bullet. It was a Knockblast shell. They didn't blow a hole through you so much as they did *inside* you, and they hit with enough force to knock out a camel.

I lifted my eyes while keeping completely still. Sure enough, Brazen was on his back.

"Brazen," Kix yelled right before the gun sounded again, followed by another thump and a thud.

The only two left were me and Reaper. Jax might have been curious about how Reaper had the funky eyes, and could have thought him immortal, but unless he had some pretty deep intel on me, he had to have assumed me dead.

Hopefully.

I gritted my teeth as I felt the disc in my back rebuilding itself. It was all I could do not to scream in pain. But I held it together.

"Now *you* are a bit of an anomaly," Jax said, walking toward Reaper. "Your glowing eyes caught me off guard when we met at the restaurant, but I overheard Gallien speaking with Haley. You're a reaper, right?"

Reaper did not reply. He was either too weak, or he wasn't about to humor the little knob.

Jax leaned down and knocked Reaper's hat off before grabbing him by his hair and lifting his head up.

"I asked you a question," Jax fumed.

"Screw you," whispered Reaper in response.

Jax let go, stood back up, and then swung a fierce kick against Reaper's jaw, knocking him out again.

"I wonder how immortal a headless reaper would be?" Jax asked as he walked back in my direction.

I closed my eyes and began to feel rage building up inside me.

"What would you think, Azura?"

"This is no time for games, Jax," answered the woman who was supposedly his wife. "Keller will be waiting."

Keller?

My mind fully engaged at that. I'd heard that name before, but I couldn't place it. Something in the back of my brain was screaming at me about it, though. Was it a case I'd worked on or studied? Damn, it actually *hurt* my head to think about it.

"He'll wait another moment," Jax argued.

I then heard the sound of steel. Like a blade was being pulled from a scabbard.

He stepped past me again.

Sure enough, he was holding a sword. I didn't know where he got it, but he sure as hell had it.

There was a sizzling feeling that made me wince something fierce. It was the completion of my healing. I was ready to move, and I wasn't about to wait.

I jumped up, spun around and kicked Azura in the chest, sending her back into the wall behind her.

"What are you doing, Azur—" was all Jax got out as he turned around and realized I wasn't dead.

The blood drained from his face.

"Hi, nutsack," I said as I punched him in the neck with my left hand while grabbing his wrist with my right. With a tight spin, driving my hip into his midsection, I flipped his ass onto his back and wrenched his arm with enough power to rip ligaments.

His anguished cry told me I'd succeeded.

The sword fell to the ground with a clang.

I kicked it away and pulled out my gun, sticking the barrel end right on his forehead.

"Do it," he said, his eyes full of tears and anger. "Kill me, you pointless bitch."

I'm not going to lie. I wanted to pull the trigger. Seriously, I *wanted* to pull the trigger. This guy had toyed with me and my crew like a pro. He'd made fools of us, and it looked like he'd even managed to kill Brazen and Kix. On top of that, he'd just been about to behead Reaper.

But I couldn't do it. Jax had used the name Keller, and the burning in my brain signaled that name was paramount to…something. Whoever he was, I *needed* to find him.

I pulled Jax to his feet by his hair, giving him a taste of the medicine he'd fed to Reaper.

"I'm not going to kill you, Jax," I hissed in his ear. "I may beat you silly and make you *wish* you were dead, but you're going to prison for damn sure."

"Ooh, I'm shaking."

"You will be," I said flatly, readying my fist for a solid punch to his stones.

"Piper," I heard Reaper say, "let him go."

Reaper was back on his feet. He was swaying back and forth, but he was up.

"I'm not going to kill him, Reap," I said with a growl. "I want him and his lovely bride to…" I turned back to find that Azura was gone. "Shit," I said, letting go of Jax while working my tattoo to see if I could spot Azura's whereabouts.

No dice.

She was completely gone and it didn't seem that she had the same kind of tattoos as the others. That meant we couldn't track her.

That's when I heard a massive whooshing sound, a brief yelp, and the sound of a body slumping to the floor.

It was Jax.

He was dead.

"What the hell…" I started, thinking that maybe he'd bitten into one of those pills like Gunter had. Then I looked up to see the look of determination on Reaper's face. "Did you just kill him?"

Reaper's eyes stayed on the body of Jax. "Yes."

"What the fuck, Reap?" I yelled. "He had information about the mage who I'm guessing was powering these runes!" I winced at the voice in my head.

Reaper blinked and then glanced at me.

"Damn it," he said with a groan. "I didn't know."

"Regardless, what about all that 'I need the entire commission' crap anyway?" I ridiculed him while pointing at Jax. "You give me shit about killing perps and then you took out the holy grail!"

"He needed killing," Reaper replied evenly.

"What, are you from the South now?" I was beside myself with rage. "You just completely fucked our chances of getting to the mage who powered these runes, Reap. Thanks a bunch."

He didn't reply.

Brazen started moaning.

Reaper stepped over and dropped down, ripping open the man's shirt to reveal he was wearing a vest. He pulled open Kix's to find the same thing as Kix lurched up and began to cough.

So the Knockblast shots put them both out, but the vests saved their asses.

I sighed in relief that nobody from my squad had been escorted away by Reaper's race that day.

But I wasn't happy about losing the two people who knew about this Keller person. My head throbbed again with the thought of that name. We must have been put under some kind of spell regarding him. I wouldn't doubt it, considering how mages could be the biggest bung masters ever.

At least Azura was still alive, wherever the hell she was. If we eventually found her, we might be able to locate her other half and take them both down at the same time.

Somehow I doubted that.

CHAPTER 30

*B*razen and Kix were in a stint with Dr. Hale. They'd been wearing vests, but the Knockblast shots could mess with your head for days if you didn't get proper attention.

Reaper was also on the road to recovery. He had a bottle of ibuprofen sitting on his desk and he was staring at it.

"Junkie," I chided before putting a call in to Pecker.

"Pecker here."

"What was the name of the wizard who drew the rune I sent down to you?" I asked, knowing full well what he was going to say.

"I don't know. Starts with an 'A,' I think. One sec."

"Azura?"

"Yeah, that's it. How'd you know?"

"I met her today."

"No kidding?"

I ignored the question. "We didn't catch her," I added

while giving a sidelong glance at Reaper, "but at least we know who's drawing these things."

Something told me I also knew who was powering them, but that painful voice in my head told me to keep that information under wraps for now.

"I gotta run, Pecker. Thanks for the help."

"No problem," he said and then added, "Listen, Piper, I'm sorry about that comment regarding your torn shirt. I've been thinking about it and it wasn't cool for me to say that."

This caught me by surprise. "Oh, uh, okay. Thanks."

"So are we good?"

"Sure, yeah. We're fine."

"Great," he said, sounding relieved. "Any chance you want to go out for drinks or something, then? You know what they say, 'Once you go Goblin, the next day you'll be hobblin.'"

I sighed and hung up as the chief waved at me from his office.

"Chief wants us," I informed Reaper as I headed off to Carter's office. "What's up, Chief?"

"I did some digging on this Azura woman you mentioned," he answered, motioning for us to take a seat. "Seems she was a wizard who was terrorizing both the Netherworld and the Overworld a little over twenty years ago." He flicked the paper he was holding. "She was captured and brought up on charges, but she got away."

I nodded. "And now she's getting herself back in the game."

"Looks like it."

"We'll just have to keep an eye out for her," I stated.

"I'm sure she'll surface again soon enough. Once they get the naughtiness bug going again, they can't seem to quit."

"No arguing that." The chief looked at me. "Tell me, how did Brazen and Kix do?"

Here was the moment of truth for those guys. On the one hand, I didn't like the idea of throwing a couple of mortals into the mix when it came to being Retrievers; on the other hand, it was likely that the chief assigned cases based on the level of power and protection his Retrievers had. They weren't exactly safe walking the beat as cops anyway. Besides, it was their choice to do this or not.

"Honestly," I answered after letting out a long breath, "they did a lot better than I would have expected."

The chief seemed surprised by this. "Really?"

"Yeah, Chief. Really."

He nodded, pulled out a slip of paper and pushed it over to me.

"Well enough to put your signature on that form?"

I looked down and saw both officers' names filled in on the Retriever Training Program application. Under "Recommending Officer" it read "Piper Shaw." That didn't exactly give me the warm and fuzzies.

But, I signed it anyway.

"Great." He tucked the document in an envelope and reached back to shove it into a tube. There was a *fwump* sound and the envelope disappeared. The chief turned to his computer and added, "I'll get them assigned to RTP training starting immediately." He tapped in one-finger style on his keyboard for a minute. "There. All set."

Well, good for Brazen and Kix.

And good for me, too.

RTP training tended to last a couple of weeks, which would keep Brazen out of my hair until then. Plus, they'd likely get assigned to handle small-time runners. Retrievers had to crawl up the ladder, just like everyone else, after all.

"I guess that's it for now," the chief said. "Commissions are in your accounts. You didn't get any full payouts, but since you ended up dragging down a number of players who have been missing for a while, it'll probably be a nice payday for you both."

Reaper seemed to sigh in relief.

"Thanks, Chief," we both said as we walked out.

CHAPTER 31

*B*razen and Kix were back at their desks when we returned, and they were all smiles. Obviously they'd seen their acceptance notifications from the chief.

After what we'd just been through, I was shocked they still wanted in. Then again, I'd felt the same way back when I started.

"Thanks, Piper," Brazen said with a gleam in his eye. "Honestly didn't expect you to have my back."

"Just trying to get you two buffoons out of my hair," I said, smirking. Then added, "Seriously, though, you guys did a good job. You deserve the chance at this." I pointed at them both. "Just don't fuck it up and make me look bad. My name is on that recommendation."

They grabbed their new coats and headed down the aisle toward the training stations.

"They're not wasting any time," noted Reaper.

"Can't blame them," I replied.

We sat in silence for a few minutes, which gave me

time to pick through emails and look at the perp boards. Nothing overly exciting was going on, but there'd be something up soon. There always was.

"Piper," Reaper said, "why didn't you bring up our partnership with the chief?"

I sat back in my chair and looked over at him, wishing we had a partition between us.

"Because everything turned out okay," I answered. "You're still a royal pain in the ass, Reap, but what's the point in dumping you now? Carter will likely just drop a fresh pain in the ass on me instead."

Reaper grinned. "Better the pain in the ass you know than the pain in the ass you don't, eh?"

"Something like that."

"So we're going to remain partners for good, then?"

I looked at him. He *did* have some pretty impressive skills. And while he made me hesitate at first, he ended up becoming an asset as the case went on.

"I guess so," I answered, shrugging.

He grinned. "Damn."

Obviously he'd taken an ibuprofen. Of all the partners I could get sidled with, mine had to be one who got stoned on basic painkillers.

"Now what do we do?" he asked. "I'm guessing we're going to hunt for Azura?"

"We'll keep an eye out for her, definitely," I answered, looking away in thought. I glanced back at him a moment later. "Reap, have you ever heard of Keller?"

In response, his smile faded and his eyes went full high-beam.

"I'm guessing you have heard of him, then?"

He nodded slowly.

"Anything you'd care to share, Reap?"

"Not a lot," he said, peering up at me. "He was a mage who did some pretty awful things in the late eighties and early nineties." He shrugged. "There's not much more I can say about it."

I nodded at him, figuring the name would eventually click.

For now I had to get some food and rest. Contrary to popular belief, fighting bad guys wasn't exactly leisurely.

"See you tomorrow, Reap."

"Have a good evening, Piper."

I walked out, thinking that maybe having him around as a partner wasn't so awful. It was damn sure better than getting stuck with someone like Brazen.

That thought made me shudder.

~

The End

~

Thanks for Reading

If you enjoyed this book, would you please leave a review at the site you purchased it from? It doesn't have to be a book report… just a line or two would be fantastic and it would really help us out!

John P. Logsdon
www.JohnPLogsdon.com

John was raised in the MD/VA/DC area. Growing up, John had a steady interest in writing stories, playing music, and tinkering with computers. He spent over 20 years working in the video games industry where he acted as designer, programmer, and producer on many online games. He's now a full-time comedy author focusing on urban fantasy, science fiction, fantasy, Arthurian, and GameLit. His books are racy, crazy, contain adult themes and language, are filled with innuendo, and are loaded with snark. His motto is that he writes stories for mature adults who harbor seriously immature thoughts.

Christopher P. Young

Chris grew up in the Maryland suburbs. He spent the majority of his childhood reading and writing science fiction and learning the craft of storytelling. He worked as a designer and producer in the video games industry for a number of years as well as working in technology and admin services. He enjoys writing both serious and comedic science fiction and fantasy. Chris lives with his wife and an ever-growing population of critters.

CRIMSON MYTH PRESS

Crimson Myth Press offers more books by this author as well as books from a few other hand-picked authors. From science fiction & fantasy to adventure & mystery, we bring the best stories for adults and kids alike.

www.CrimsonMyth.com